The Luxembourg Rose Deception

A Sister Gilmary Thriller

Second in the series

Mary Klovers

Castle Ellis
Publishing

Division of Butler Properties, LLC

The Luxembourg Rose Deception is a sequel to the first Sister Gilmary thriller, *Casting a Shadow over Rome.*

Cover photo: Jorge Royan, *Backlit Red Rose with Water Droplets,* Wikimedia

Dedication

This novel is dedicated to Mary Louise, who played Watson to my Holmes, as well as to Karen, Betty and Ruth. Our exploits many years ago are fodder for my imagination today.

Special thanks to Michael for editing advice.

Introduction

The Cold War (1946–1989) between the USSR and the United States and Western Europe engendered many covert operations. One of the most secret of these was Operation Gladio which began in 1952 as a joint effort of the NATO countries to create clandestine "stay-behind" armies in fourteen of its member nations. The task of these secret armies was to gather intelligence, secure hidden caches of weapons, train a local clandestine army and plan citizen escape routes in case of a Soviet invasion. A great deal of the planning and execution of Operation Gladio was carried out by the United States CIA and MI6 of the United Kingdom.

The existence of Gladio did not come to public attention until 1990, just after the end of the Cold War. Even to this day, hidden caches of weapons belonging to the local "stay-behind" armies are being discovered in unlikely places.

Chapter One

Capo di Marrargui, Sardinia
March 25, 1965

Olga Dicderich's first act of freedom was to look west across the deep indigo waters of the Mediterranean Sea. She sighed with relief. The sun had descended enough for shadows to obscure the rocky crevices of the sharp drop-off before her. Those lengthening shadows mushrooming over the face of the cliff would also obscure her movements and those of her two companions.

In front of her and down towards the sea, his image blurred by mist and the encroaching dusk, Uri was already carefully descending the rough, shallow steps that peasants or fishermen had hewn in the cliff face countless centuries ago. Squelching her impatience at his slow pace, she bit her lip and peered up at Ivan. His ungainly, stocky frame was outlined against the darkening sky. On his left shoulder he balanced a thick coil of rope, while he spat out small grunting noises as he let his heavy frame sink into each step.

Above them Olga could hear the constant, irritating gong of the prison alarm. As soon as the riot started, it had activated. She wished the three of them could have made their escape without such fanfare, but it was impossible.

Two weeks before, she had laid the groundwork for the riot and their escape. It wasn't difficult. She started with a whispering campaign to the other prisoners in the exercise yard that fellow prisoners were systematically being eliminated. Surely their numbers seemed to shrink perceptibly every day. Where they went she didn't know, but she suspected it was into solitary confinement to soften them up for more interrogation.

It served her purpose, nevertheless, to tell the others that she had seen dead bodies being carried out at night. They believed her, and their panic grew until it spilled over into a riot. To the guards, it seemed as if the rumpus began spontaneously in the exercise yard, then multiplied in intensity and spread to the cellblocks like a fast-moving virus, until the noise shook the walls and filled every dark crevice of the prison. While the others were creating mayhem, she and the two hefty Russians had made their escape.

The only serious glitch in her plan was the blocking of the main prison entrance by a whole phalanx of guards who were positioned there so the prisoners could not escape onto the high plateau and disappear into the wilds of Sardinia. She had thought the guards would be positioned around the cell blocks and exercise yard. However, it appeared that none of the guards considered that anyone would try to escape to the sea. It would be too treacherous and the escapees would only get trapped on the beach between rocks and the churning waves.

Leading her two fellow prisoners on a quick detour, Olga had found the thick metal barrier that separated them from the narrow back entrance which led down to the sea. She'd only needed Uri and Ivan to jimmy the electric doors and hold them open with their heavy, muscular bodies while the three of them forced their way out of the cell block.

Once outside the prison wall, Olga drew in a deep, heady draft of the fresh, damp sea air. As her head cleared, it dawned on her that the prison break was the easy part; what lay ahead would be the real challenge.

Now on the beach, she and the other two Soviet agents made their way four hundred feet south. The waves were already nipping at their feet and filling in their footprints. Stopping at a spot where an outcropping of rock jutted out ten feet above their heads, they could just make out the top of the cliff eighty feet further up.

Olga commanded Ivan to hand her the rope. "I'll make the first ascent and secure the rope to some stable rock above us. Then you, Ivan, will climb next. Both of you must start on that stone outcrop above us because the cable's not long enough otherwise."

The two men nodded their assent slow-wittedly. It was natural for her to call the shots. Wasn't she the one who designed their escape? Without her they had no viable plan.

Olga continued, "As Ivan's climbing the rope, you, Uri, must stand directly below him, holding the cable to stabilize his climb. Then it will be your turn, and we'll help you up."

Turning to the rock face, Olga began her ascent with the rope slung over her shoulder. She was an adept climber, having practiced as a teenager in the Elbe Sandstone Mountains of East Germany. Moments later she reached the summit and secured the rope to a solid chunk of rock. Before long the cord stretched taut under the weight of the larger man.

Peering down toward the churning waves that had now engulfed the whole beach, she could just make out the bulk of the two men, one directly under the other. Slowly Ivan climbed the rock face, using the rope to secure his balance. His weight impeded his progress, but now he was only thirty feet from the top. Breathing in labored gasps between lips stretched into an excruciating grimace while placing his right foot on a stable plateau of granite, he paused to wipe sweat from his brow. Then, after looking up to gauge the distance to the end of his dangerous climb, he again prepared to put all of his weight on the rope.

Olga marveled at his trust of her. At the top of the cliff, slowly and carefully she had begun sliding the end of the cord through its own loop. Each time Ivan let the rope slacken, as he rested with a precarious perch on the rocks, she loosened it more.

Now the exhausted Russian stepped off his perch and pulled on the rope. This time there was no resistance. Tumbling backward while grasping the slack cord in desperation, he let out a horrible, guttural scream just as the weight of thirty-five feet of rope fell upon him with a thud.

Directly below him, Uri jerked his head up only to see Ivan hurdling down toward him. There was no time to react and jump into the waves below. Both men smashed heavily onto the rocky ledge.

Olga heard their terrible moans, but deftly rose and turned away from the sea. As of this moment her new life began. She was free! Too bad about Uri and Ivan. She had never intended for them to escape with her since the three of them making their way across Sardinia would be too conspicuous. By herself, however, she knew she could do it.

As the clouds cleared enough for the moon to illuminate the scene before her, Olga saw all around her rough terrain hemmed in by low mountains on the horizon. Behind her lay the Capo di Marrargui, the forbidding locale for the Operation Gladio prison, where the CIA and its associates secreted away the Soviet spies they snared in their nets. It was the hell she was escaping from.

She herself had been captured in Rome last May. That her capture had taken place in St. Peter's Basilica on the day of the pope's audience seemed almost sacrilegious. Of course, she was an atheist, so nothing about Rome or anywhere else was sacred. But hadn't she been dressed as a Dominican nun in a place swarming with men and women in religious garb? For the longest time she wondered how the CIA had known she was an impostor. No one at the Regina Coeli Hospital had challenged her because of her disguise the night she killed the Italian journalist.

But now she knew. Fritz Eichel, the debonair Fritz who had trained with her in East Berlin three years ago, was the turncoat. Why he would snitch on another agent puzzled her. More than puzzling her, it pained her—especially because he seemed to lavish all of his attention on her when they spent time together. But she hadn't seen him again since the day their assignments were posted—hers to Rome and his to Turin in the north of Italy. Not that she had forgotten him. In fact, she had held the memory of him close to her heart and had hoped he still cherished his moments with her. Now, however, the thought of him seared her emotions as painfully as a fresh stab wound.

Three years ago, as a well-trained East German Stasi assassin working for the Soviets, she had felt ready to prove herself in Rome. And hadn't she been successful in eliminating the journalist who was about to publish an expose on a communist plot? Unfortunately for her, she'd been picked up by the CIA before she could do the really big job—poisoning the head of the Christian Democrat party.

Suddenly ahead of her she glimpsed a light. It bobbed and swayed in the darkness. Crouching behind a rock, Olga listened intently. "*Cluck, cluck,*" chickens were being disturbed. Moving closer, the escapee could make out an old woman coming around the side of a low hut. It was she who held the bobbing lantern.

"*Chi, chi, chi,*" she whispered to her fryers. "*Su, su!*" But proving she had a soft spot for her hens, the old woman took a metal cup from a rough wooden box balanced on rocks a couple of feet above the ground. Olga could hear the rough, pebbly sound as the woman slid the cup into the box. Soon the hens awakened excitedly and scrambled for kernels of corn. Chuckling in satisfaction, the woman replaced the cup and closed the box. With shambling steps, she turned with her lantern swaying before her and retreated back inside her hut.

Olga advanced towards the feed box while the chickens in their pen were still scratching for kernels. Quickly she scooped up a large cup of corn and disappeared around the hut. If she soaked the kernels in water, she could chew them when she became desperately hungry.

"Thwack!" Unexpectedly, something soft slapped her face in the gloom. Stepping back abruptly, she let out a deep breath and relaxed, relieved that it was only clothes hanging on a line. Quickly she grabbed a man's shirt, pants and a pillow case. Then she silently scrambled down the path away from the hut.

Ahead she saw a pale light spreading brightness across the night sky. Probably it was the feebly reflected light from the town of Bosa. Months before, she had traveled to the prison with a hood over her head, but by slowly mining the local guards for information she'd found out she was in an isolated, rocky corner of Sardinia. The nearest town was a small fishing port called Bosa. She surmised they called it Bosa, which reminded her of the Italian word for mouth, because, like a mouth next to its sandy beach, there its river emptied into the sea. That same sea would be her route away from her imprisonment she desperately hoped.

Two hours later found her stretched out uncomfortably under a canoe that had been pulled ashore and left overturned in the deep shadows under the only bridge in the small town. Fifty feet behind her a dozen motorboats and an equal number of fishing boats rocked lazily in the slow moving water. These craft were too large and noisy for her purposes. Already men, searching with lanterns, had gone on board each boat so she knew they were looking for her. No, this inconspicuous canoe cloaked in inky shadows hid her perfectly.

"Clang, clang." It was two o'clock in the morning; the bell in the village tower pealed twice—a dissonant, hollow sound. There were no other sounds or movement except a stealthy

6

shadow creeping next to the water under the bridge. Slowly Olga worked the canoe to the water and swung it into the river. Then she quietly slipped into it and paddled towards the sea.

Although fatigue threatened to overtake her, it felt exhilarating to have the sea breeze slide across her face and tickle her cheeks. Now the waves swelled more gently than they had five hours ago, so there seemed little chance of her capsizing. Fortunately, slow-moving clouds intermittently covered the moon. It only showed its face often enough for her to make out the outline of rocks in the shallows near the shore.

She paddled north along the coast, far enough out to avoid skirting too close to the prison shore. At the base of the cliff, where she'd climbed just a few hours ago, a searchlight traced an arc while it probed the rough crevices of the cliff. Watching the light swing up and down and back and forth, Olga thought with satisfaction that they would never turn their light towards the sea. The March chill and the frigid water would deter anyone except the most intrepid.

Another grain of information she'd gleaned from a guard concerned the Grotto di Netunno. An extensive labyrinth of natural inlets and caves, it featured enormous stalactites, stalagmites and the deepest turquoise water. To the native Sardinians, the grotto was a source of pride and revenue since several tourist boats motored out every day from Alghero, a town near the northern coast of the island, facing Corsica. If she could find the grotto, she had a plan to further her escape. All she needed was the stamina to keep her sore back and aching arms paddling against the growing swell of the waves.

Chapter Two

Aalsmeer, the Netherlands
April 12, 1965

Red, pink and purple. Mauve, orange and scarlet. And those were only the hues of the red flowers! The next train of carts held all the shades of blue and yellow blooms. This kaleidoscope of moving colors in the Aalsmeer Flower Auction was giving Sister Gilmary a headache.

It wasn't just the dizzying variety of colors; it was the way the drivers of the carts chose to zig-zag about so the audience of buyers and spectators could view their colorful wares. But how did the men behind the wheels of these carts keep from bumping into each other and spilling their blooms? It seemed like a crazy Indy 500 race, but with no discernible track.

Sister Gilmary's gaze wandered off to the gallery on her right where the buyers, all men, were bidding on the flowers using the Dutch auction method. For several of the foreign observers, this type of auction seemed topsy-turvy. The director of the auction would announce a number and letter for a specific cartload and suggest a high price as a starting bid rather than a low number. Perhaps it indicated how much they valued their blooms. Today, however, this group of buyers seemed especially conservative. Most of them didn't enter the competitive bidding until the numbers had dropped precipitously. Then their bare-knuckled bidding became animated. After all, why pay a high price for your flowers if you could get them cheap enough to make more profit for yourself and the florists.

Looking to her left and down her row of spectators, she saw the ladies of the Luxembourg Rosarian Society were relaxed and enjoying the auction of tulips, lilies and daffodils, but only exhibiting moderate enthusiasm. Next to her, Gilmary's mother, the current president of the society, was reading the information booklet they'd been given on their tour. Turning to her daughter, Genevieve Andrews smiled and pointed to an especially vivid cartload of tulips.

"Wouldn't it be lovely to have a garden full of those in the spring? Maybe I should put a flowerbed of yellow tulips in front of the Melucina fountain."

Gilmary cocked her head as she considered. "Well, since the character of Melusina is part human and part fish, it seems like blue flowers would be more fitting, with a few white flowers popping up here and there like the sun's rays dancing over the waves."

"Yes, I can visualize that," responded her mother with a shake of her head.

Just then the double, extra-large, metal doors to the staging area opened. All eyes turned towards the carts which were now exiting. Finally the moment the Luxembourgish ladies had been waiting for! The backs of the wooden chairs creaked as ten ladies craned forward in anticipation of seeing the most beautiful flower in the world—the rose!

Gilmary also moved forward in her chair and strained to see the train of carts coming towards them. But suddenly she focused on two men conspicuously dressed in business suits and only visible for a moment when the extra-wide metal doors swung open. All of the other workers at the flower auction wore utilitarian overalls. Incredibly, the grey-haired, older man in a dark suit looked like Arthur Leventhal, thought the young nun with surprise. And his gaze also seemed to be arrested when he looked towards the gallery of spectators. In fact, he appeared to be looking directly at Gilmary and her mother.

"Mother, did you see those two businessmen back there in the warehouse when the doors opened? One looked just like Arthur Leventhal. What would he be doing here?"

"Oh, it couldn't be Arthur, dear. I don't think he has any interest in gardening or flowers. Besides, didn't you tell me that he's the CIA chief in Rome?"

Gilmary still kept staring at the metal doors now closed after divulging their load of flower carts. The wagons, overflowing with extravagant quantities of roses, swirled before them making the rose society ladies swoon with a feeling of nirvana—such was their delight. But Gilmary was missing the feeling as she pondered the mystery of Mr. Leventhal. Probably her mother was right. Arthur wouldn't have any business here. He was too busy fighting the Cold War back in Italy.

After the last cart of flowers had been bought and rolled away to be shipped to some floral broker, the spectators started to gather up their belongings and parade off the viewing floor. Advancing towards the rose society ladies, though, came a dapper young man carrying a box of bouquets under one arm and waving his free arm like an orchestra conductor. "Ladies, ladies, please sit down for a moment. I have something to say to you!" the young man exclaimed with a pleasant smile.

After the matrons had resumed their seats, the auction representative said, "I hear we've had the pleasure of hosting the Luxembourg Rosarian Society this morning. We hope you're enjoying your visit. Our roses today are especially fine, so we want to present each of you with a small bouquet for your pleasure."

The ladies became animated, murmuring delightfully about what a wonderful time they were having, and weren't the roses the loveliest. The young man then handed each a small bouquet of three harmoniously-hued blooms with their stems wrapped in green floral paper. Only a single bouquet

10

distinctively wrapped in pink paper still lay in the box. Turning to Gilmary, he presented it to her with a bow.

Genevieve and Gilmary smiled appreciatively as they sniffed the faint, delicate odor of the roses. Suddenly, Gilmary let out a small yelp as she pricked her finger on a thorn. Looking closely into the bouquet, she spied a small twist of blue paper, which she drew out.

Putting down her flowers, she unraveled the paper and read, "Isaac Paredes Diamonds, 10 Weesperstraat, 12:30".

Oh no, not another cryptic message! The last one, which she'd been handed several months ago by a widow draped in black in the middle of the piazza of St. Peter's Basilica in Rome, had launched her into an adventure she'd like to forget. Arthur Leventhal had played a major role in that adventure, so she hoped she'd been mistaken about the identity of the older man they'd glimpsed today in the warehouse.

Genevieve Andrews noticed her daughter's quiet preoccupation. Peering over her shoulder, she read the small piece of paper. "That's for me, dear," she said, reaching for the note.

Gilmary looked sharply at her mother. "I don't think so! I think it's someone's idea of advertising. They think we're flush enough with money to want to go diamond shopping while we're in Amsterdam. Who can be daft enough to think a nun would be buying a diamond."

"That's why I think it's for me."

"Oh Mom, diamonds for you? You hardly wear any jewelry. It's not your style. You're dignified and elegant enough without glitter."

Her mother smiled gently. "Thanks for the compliment, daughter I think, however, that I'll visit the Paredes shop while you're all having lunch. Just don't tell the others where I am. They might think I'm getting high-falutin' ideas."

"No, no, you aren't leaving me with all of those ladies.

They'll be comparing notes on the grand accomplishments of their precious offspring. I'll have nothing to add to the conversation. I may as well go with you and find out how diamonds go from rough, dull stones to the stuff of legend."

At half past twelve, which was a little early for lunch, the two Andrews ladies stood on Weesperstraat in front of a window displaying gorgeous diamonds. On the other side to the right of the door, was another corresponding window surrounded by a bevy of milling, inquisitive tourists. What Gilmary and her mother could barely see over the heads of the crowd was a man in white shirtsleeves with a jeweler's loupe resembling a monocle held tightly to his right eye. He was concentrating on cutting facets into a diamond in spite of the constant movement of the shifting crowd before him. One could only admire his single-mindedness.

Upon entering the store, the two women wondered what to do next. They'd been summoned here, but didn't know by whom.

Almost immediately, a young man wearing a yamulka over his slicked-back hair looked their way. His gaze seemed to have been drawn to Sister Gilmary's white Dominican habit. Approaching them, he took each by their elbow and steered them towards the back room. Speaking rather loudly and addressing Mrs. Andrews, he said that he had a special necklace to show her and would they please come this way.

As soon as the door to the back of the shop had closed behind them, his demeanor changed. All businesslike, he hustled them down a corridor and opened the entrance to the basement stairway.

Uncertain and confused, Gilmary and her mother looked questioningly at the young man. He smiled his encouragement and urged them forward. Now as they descended the stairs, they could see a large room with ample light coming into view. Then they noticed a spacious desk in the center of the basement room, and standing up behind it and ready to welcome them, was Arthur Leventhal.

"Arthur!" gasped Mrs. Andrews.

"Genevieve, or should I say Madame von Hollenden as you are known in Luxembourg City," answered Leventhal with an engaging smile. For as such Genevieve Andrews, a widow, was called in Luxembourg, where her family had resided for centuries before she had married Steven Andrews and moved to the United States.

"Oh Arthur, you know we're not so formal." And with that they greeted each other warmly with a kiss on each cheek.

Gilmary stood dumb-founded with her mouth hanging open. Coming over to her, the distinguished, older man came and kissed the young sister on each cheek too. Gilmary was too shocked to respond properly. Incredible! Arthur and her mother seemed to know each other better than she thought.

Wasn't their last meeting more than a dozen years ago when Arthur had helped the family relocate from Florence, Italy back to the States? It happened during the chaotic time immediately after her father had been murdered by a Soviet assassin. At that time Arthur had been attached to the American Consulate in Florence, just like her father.

After they were all seated and served a cup of coffee, Arthur leaned back in his chair, clasped his hands behind his head and beamed amiably at them both.

"You know, you really do stand out in a crowd wearing that white habit. Even among the decoration of the Luxembourg Rosarian Society ladies, you're like a beacon. I consider it fortuitous to see you in Aalsmeer today and even better to have you here now. Thank you for coming," Arthur said with a small bow of his head.

His graciousness is really quite disarming, thought

Gilmary, totally taken in by his charm.

Having finished his introduction, Arthur leaned forward and started his careful campaign to enlist their aid in his latest assault on the Soviet's European plan.

"Genevieve, as the president of the Luxembourg Rosarian Society, I believe you are in a unique position to aid the cause of European freedom. Tell me about what your society does."

Genevieve leaned forward too and warmed to her subject as she explained the mission of the group. After all, it wasn't often that anyone asked about their agenda.

"Very few people realize that Luxembourg in the 19th century was known as the 'Garden of the North' for roses. Would you believe it? Our varieties were famous all over the world, from St. Petersburg to South America. A large number of the roses originating in our country were exported to famous and not-so-famous gardens in every corner of Europe. Now that we've rebuilt our country after the war, we can concentrate on enhancing our cultural heritage. Bringing home slips from heirloom Luxembourg roses in far-flung gardens and welcoming them lovingly back into native gardens is the society's idea of promoting our horticultural heritage. Every time we bring back a slip of a rose, it's as if we are repatriating a child."

Gilmary looked at her mother appreciatively. She took pride in her work, and felt that it truly did enhance their people's sense of self-worth.

Arthur could admire the sentiment behind the ladies' efforts too, but he had a different and more pressing agenda. Clasping his hands tightly in front of him on the desk so that the knuckles appeared white, he leaned forward and zeroed in with a solemn gaze at the two women.

"Do you know how many days it took for Nazi Germany to overrun Norway in 1940?" Both ladies, surprised by the sudden shift in the conversation and his abrupt gravitas, sat mute while Arthur continued. "Only little more than a day. And what

14

about little Luxembourg? Your people suffered under the heel of the Third Reich from the spring of 1940 through the spring of 1945." Arthur spoke solemnly. "It took a superhuman effort for the Allies to overcome the well-oiled Nazi war machine."

Genevieve lowered her eyes, remembering how her parents and others suffered. It had been a cruel, terrifying nightmare for thousands of Luxemburgers. Fortunately, she and her husband and their children were living in the States during those years. In 1950, however, when they moved to Florence so her husband could work at the American Consulate, Europe was still rebuilding. Not just physical scars needed healing then, but psychological wounds too.

Arthur continued. "After the war, the people of Europe, that is, the countries of the continent that had not fallen under Soviet control, vowed never to be caught again so unprepared. They had become complacent in the years following World War I and up until World War II. Maybe they were just exhausted. For whatever reason, when Hitler rose to power in the 1930s and threatened his neighbors' sovereignty, they cowered before the military strength of the Third Reich. So when they ought to have slain the dragon, they instead appeased it."

Gilmary shifted in her chair. The mood of Arthur's soliloquy weighed heavily; too somber for what had started out as a carefree day as a tourist.

Now with his preamble over, Arthur approached the meat of his message in a lower voice. "You probably have never heard of Operation Gladio. And you never should have. It's a super-secret army in Italy that operates totally in the shadows of society. It means to ensure that if the Soviets try to enter Italy with their army they will meet insurmountable resistance. If this group were publically acknowledged, the communists, already suspecting something, would actively declare war on it.

"You see, the Soviets, who at present tightly control all of Eastern Europe, desperately want to extend their iron grip to Italy.

After that, it is on to Greece and eventually Scandinavia, France and all the rest of Europe. The socialist appetite is never satiated. World domination's their aim, and they'll employ every unethical means to achieve it."

Genevieve and her daughter were solemnly impressed. Tensely, Gilmary spoke. "I can attest to their ruthlessness. After all, when I impersonated Olga Diederich, the Stasi assassin, in the plot against Aldo Falucci in Rome last summer, I found out how cruelly they acted. Later I had to live with those foul Russian spies in the villa in Firenze. Their souls had withered, dried up and turned to dust! If it weren't for the two children of Rosa, the housekeeper, I would've become desperately depressed. Innocently, they buoyed my spirits through it all."

A cloud passed over Arthur's face as he pondered, not for the first time, the danger in which he had placed the young and unprepared nun when she helped the CIA in Rome just a few months ago. That they were able to rescue her before the frustrated Russians had spirited her off behind the Iron Curtain was due to the determined efforts of her cousin, Emile, and her friend, Sister Maria Goretti.

Gilmary's mother, with moist eyes, put her arms around her daughter's tense shoulders. She only knew the bare outline of her daughter's ordeal in Italy last summer and fall. Thankfully, it hadn't left any shadow over her lively daughter's spirit. Thinking it would be beneficial to have Gilmary home in Luxembourg and close to her family for a few months after such an ordeal, Genevieve had petitioned her old friend, Mother Assumpta, back at the convent in Wisconsin, to allow Gilmary that privilege.

Turning back to Arthur, Genevieve eyed him suspiciously. "Arthur, I know you're a no-nonsense man. So why do you want us here for this tete-a-tete? It's nice to share a cup of coffee with you, but I feel there's a deeper reason."

The distinguished man's face lost its intensity as it wrinkled pleasantly into a smile. "Of course, Genevieve! As you can imagine, these clandestine armies need weapons. The CIA and NATO can supply most of these, but we have to keep their whereabouts secret.

"You probably wondered today why I'd suddenly taken a fancy to cut flowers at the auction in Aalsmeer. It's not merely a novel whim of mine. Those shipments of blooms can disguise our shipment of weapons. Hidden under the blooms can be rifles, ammo, and machine guns. Of course, their weight could give it away, so we need a secure sender and receiver.

"Now your travels to gardens around Europe as the representative of the Rosarian Society give you unique cover. You could be the transmitter of messages both ways—from us to the 'stay-behind' armies, as the local militias are known, and vice-versa."

Madame von Hollenden couldn't believe what she was hearing. She would become an undercover agent! Life was uncharacteristically quiet in her home now that her son, Nathan, was away at university in Paris. But did she want this kind of tension and excitement in her life? Still, it was a unique opportunity to do something for freedom during the Cold War. Did she owe it to her dead husband, who was killed by a Soviet assassin?

Gilmary could guess at the thoughts her mother was wrestling with now. She wondered how long it would take for her to come to a decision.

Before speaking, the older woman poured herself another cup of coffee. Still warm, its stimulation helped her thoughts coalesce into a decision. She would do it!

Once she had internalized the idea, Genevieve smiled warmly at Arthur. "I'm in!" she declared firmly. "After all, if my husband and daughter had the intestinal fortitude to put their lives on the line for freedom, so can I."

While the young nun watched, Arthur rose enthusiastically, left his chair to come around the desk and warmly embraced Madam von Hollenden. He had to admire the bravery of this family. They'd never retreat into a safe and comfortable hole while watching others risk their lives to protect the freedom they enjoyed.

Later on the train back to Luxembourg City, the ladies of the Rosarian Society chattered amiably about their exciting day. Only two, seated behind the others, sat lost in their own reveries. Looking at her mother, Gilmary winked and squeezed her hand. They were now co-conspirators.

Chapter Three

Grotto di Netunno, Sardinia

The twenty-five windswept tourists on the 'Capriccio' were exchanging excited exclamations as they neared the opening to the grotto. Gathering up cameras, binoculars and bags, they were carefully helped from the bobbing boat onto the narrow landing stage.

"Line up here in a single file, please," barked the guide, a young Sardinian sporting the company uniform. He briskly surveyed the chattering, excited line of tourists. After a minute in which a ragged line began to form, he led them forward on the path around the many caverns of the grotto.

From her unseen position behind a grouping of stalagmites, Olga watched the group advance. Why would some ladies insist on wearing heels even when advised not to, she thought. Before the end of their hike through the maze of sparkling corridors, at least one lady will have sprained her ankle and be complaining loudly about how the path is treacherous and uneven. Even though Olga's great passion was elegant shoes, she accepted reality when it came to wearing them.

Now the group moved closer into the caverns. Most were viewing the whole scene from the confines of their camera lenses. Olga's gaze finally settled on the last person straggling at the end of the line. She'd noticed the young woman spoke to no one and seemed completely enthralled with the beautiful subterranean scenes as they were revealed. Like the other women, she wore a blouse, full skirt and a sweater, wrapped tightly around her slender frame against the cold. Around her neck, hung binoculars and a camera. Topping it all off was a floppy straw sunhat over her blonde hair. The way she peered closely at some of the stone formations made Olga think she was nearsighted.

After all of the group had passed and turned the corner to the next grotto, the straggler came into view all alone. Before the unfortunate woman could react and scream, Olga, positioned behind her, deftly slung a sock around the woman's face and harnessed it through her mouth, twisting its ends into a tight knot. Then she secured the startled woman's wrists behind her with the sleeves of the shirt purloined from the Sardinian lady's clothesline. Through eyeglasses knocked askew, the girl's desperate eyes beseeched Olga for mercy. But Olga ignored the silent plea and punched the woman in the abdomen so she folded like an accordion, then dragged her into a secluded gap in the cavern wall and secured her legs with the Sardinian's pants. It was useless for the young tourist to resist; she was up against a trained Stasi assassin.

With a careful strike to the woman's neck, Olga knocked the woman out and roughly stripped her of her outer clothing. After dressing herself in the woman's clothes, she looked down at the unfortunate girl, whose holiday plans had just taken a turn towards disaster. She decided not to kill her by strangling. The young woman looked Germanic; it would be hard to kill a fellow Aryan, and besides, it would be some time before the girl could drag herself far enough onto the main path to be seen and get help.

Satisfied with her handiwork, Olga placed the woman's glasses on her nose and squinted. Yes, as she had suspected, the woman tourist was nearsighted. Picking up the girl's handbag and scarf, she considered that she'd have to be careful not to bump into stones and stalactites herself.

Far ahead, the group was carefully stepping into the

bobbing "Capriccio", while another gaggle of tourists disembarked from their own craft which had just arrived. Olga waved and shouted to the departing group in order to get their attention. While running to catch up, she hoped that no one had closely scrutinized the German woman on the way to the grotto. Tucking a wayward strand of auburn hair into the scarf she had tied around her head, she pulled the straw hat down so it covered the crown of her head and her hair completely.

"You almost got left behind," noted the older lady seated to her left in the swaying boat. "The grotto's lovely, but who'd want to spend the night here? After they turn the lights off, it must be cold and eerie." The lady shivered at the thought of it and then turned to continue chattering with her elderly husband about where they were going to eat dinner. Olga shrugged her shoulders and silently marveled at what she'd just gone through in the last twenty-four hours. If the older lady had known what the Stasi agent sitting so close to her had just done, she would have screamed and jumped overboard. The thought of it gave the escapee great satisfaction.

Olga rummaged through her hostage's purse and found a passport and money as well as a ferry ticket from Porto Torre back to Civitavecchio, the port closest to Rome. What luck! Opening the passport, she discovered the young German's name was Margarethe Olbeck, a teacher from Augsburg, twenty-four years old. That was only a couple of years younger than herself. It looked like a chinch to impersonate her enough to get back to Rome. And the money too! Margarethe must have just started her trip since there were enough Italian lire to last a week.

Satisfied, Olga sat back, smiled and congratulated herself. She was back in the game! But what she immediately needed was to fortify herself with a large dinner in a restaurant in Alghero. Then she'd be off to the ferry at Porto Torre and on to Rome.

Chapter Four

Luxembourg City

"I'm leaving tomorrow for Oslo, dear," Madame von Hollenden explained to her daughter as they settled into comfortable chairs on the sunny veranda. It was a rare spring day when the sun had pierced the cool dampness enough to make it a delight to sit in the garden. Opening the French doors, they had moved two chairs out from the living room, and now were relaxing as they discussed their plans.

"The Oslo Rose Garden Society has invited me to come, and I'm anxious to begin this job of finding Luxembourg roses and bringing them home." She didn't say anything about the work she would do for Arthur. Her daughter knew that it was better if they didn't speak of it.

Gilmary shaded her eyes as she glanced at her mother. "How long will you be gone?"

"Well, after I leave Norway, I may as well visit Sweden. There are a couple of promising leads there also. So it may be about three weeks before I return."

"Does Nathan know you'll be gone? In fact have you heard from him at all lately? I hope he's really studying in Paris, and not being led around with a hook through his nose by a lot of rudderless hippies," said Gilmary wrinkling her nose.

Her mother heaved a weary sigh. Her son was eighteen and in his first year of university. His was a gentle soul, easily influenced by his friends. Of course, he'd gone through his youth

22

and adolescent years without the steadiness usually provided by an attentive father. Fortunately for Gilmary, she'd known and been very close to her father for twelve years before he was killed. It showed in the altruistic and goal-driven spirit of her daughter.

"The only news I hear from Nathan is vague but reassuring. Maybe he just doesn't want me to worry about him, or maybe he's maturing into a serious student." Madame von Hollenden fervently hoped the latter was true.

"Anyway, remember dear, you won't be alone here. In a little more than a week, Sister Maria Goretti will be raiding our pantry. I stocked it well enough so even she ought to be satisfied for the few weeks while I'm away."

Gilmary grinned at the pleasurable thought of her friend and companion, who was coming from Wisconsin to join her. Since Maria Goretti had helped Emile scour Florence looking for her late last summer, she'd truly felt sisterly towards her. It would be great to have her here for a couple of months.

It was a Thursday afternoon when the telephone rang at the von Hollenden residence. Since Genevieve had left for Oslo two days before, it was Gilmary who answered.

"The von Hollenden residence. Sister Gilmary speaking."

The voice on the other end of the line hesitated, thinking he had accidently reached a convent. "Ah, hello.... Um, this is Inspector Pepin from the Paris Surete. I'm trying to reach Madame von Hollenden. It's a matter concerning her son."

With her apprehension growing Gilmary replied, "I'm afraid she's out of the country presently, but I'm the sister of Nathan Andrews."

The man on the other end of the line cleared his throat and continued. "Good. Well then, we need to communicate to

23

the family that your brother's been arrested and held in jail here in Paris."

Grasping the telephone receiver tightly, Gilmary's other hand flew to her mouth as she gasped. It had happened as she had feared. Her brother's erstwhile friends had led him into trouble. "What happened? What's he done?"

"He was part of a small band of thieves we caught stealing hubcaps and spray painting communist slogans on public buildings. Until his arraignment, he's being held in the central city jail. It would certainly be helpful if a family member could come to Paris to help us sort this out."

Without pausing for more details, Gilmary responded decisively. "Of course I'll come! You can expect me tomorrow."

Sitting together in a drab interrogation room, the siblings looked equally sad. Nathan, his lean frame slumped in a wooden chair with his head hanging down, was unwilling to meet his sister's eyes. Gilmary stared at her younger brother, who looked pale and frightened. Her heart went out to him, but at the same time she felt exasperated with his foolishness. If only their father were here to guide them. She'd never regretted his absence before as painfully as she did now.

Since they had already hashed out the situation as much as they could today, Gilmary sighed, stood and hugged her brother. Whether from embarrassment or self-pity, Nathan wiped tears from his troubled eyes.

"I'll be back tomorrow," said his sister. "I'm going to pray about this, and you'd better do the same!" she demanded firmly.

After walking a few blocks away from the jail, Gilmary saw a church that was open and entered the dark, cool interior. Sitting in the stillness, she contemplated what to do next. Who could help her and Nathan?

The first image coming to mind was her many-talented cousin, Emile. The twenty-one-year old, who off and on supported himself as an entertainer, was now enrolled here in Paris at the Chez Maison Desiree Cooking School. He fancied himself an inspired chef after working last summer with Sister Bona in the Villa Rosa kitchen in Rome. His presence there in a convent, necessitated by his need to be hidden from unknown pursuers, meant he had to disguise himself as a Dominican nun. Such was his talent that what had seemed unlikely had actually worked.

But springing Nathan from jail would necessitate a different talent. She really didn't think Emile had anything but good will to offer to this enterprise. Nevertheless, since she was in Paris, she had better look him up.

Emile was just leaving his last class of the day at the cooking school. Hopping on his unicycle while still sporting his chef's toque over his black curls, he maneuvered the cycle into the traffic. Because he'd let his hair grow long and wore it tied back, he felt older and more professional. After all, he was training to enter a serious profession. Visions of critical acclaim as the new face of gastronomical success filled his daydreams.

Suddenly, the sun disappeared and the sky opened to a cloudburst. Surprised, the pedestrians scurried hastily to take refuge under awnings and in doorways. Gilmary had just turned onto Rue de L'ouvain and was heading towards the sign that proclaimed "Chez Maison Desiree Cooking School" in magenta letters over a tastefully decorated display window. Incredibly, Emile was heading her way. Ignoring the rain, she stopped to admire how deftly he maneuvered the unicycle in and out of traffic. Cars honked at him, but he coolly avoided all comers. She didn't know he could even ride a unicycle, but imagined that any action demanding showmanship would appeal to him.

Putting two fingers into her mouth in a most un-lady-like manner, she whistled loudly to get his attention. Hearing the piercing sound, Emile looked sharply to his left and over the flow of cars. There, through the rain, he saw a nun in a white habit beckoning to him. Gilmary! What was she doing here? And without a sister companion again! He thought every nun was supposed to have a companion whenever they left the convent walls. Apparently, convent rules were arbitrary to his cousin.

An hour later found the two cousins sitting inside near the steamy front window of a small neighborhood bistro with their heads together and watching raindrops drip in rhythm from the awning overhanging the narrow sidewalk. Having talked themselves out over dinner, they now sat quietly contemplating the dilemma of Nathan Andrews. When they had first been seated, they eagerly interrupted each other as their words spilled out. There was so much to share since their last adventure in Rome and Florence.

Eventually, however, a pall fell over their initial enthusiasm at meeting each other. Gilmary had explained Nathan's predicament to her cousin. "He thinks he's a Maoist and that capitalism's the modern evil of his generation."

Emile interjected rather bitterly, "There are hundreds, maybe thousands of those misguided would-be anarchists all over Europe's university campuses. Instead of attending classes, they stupidly march through the streets clogging traffic and belittling any intellectual thought. You'll see their graffiti on walls all over Paris. 'Down with America!' 'Stamp out the imperialist pig!'"

Gilmary put her hand over her cousin's and said, "Yes, they forget who gave them this freedom to express their discontent. It was mainly the Americans and British who freed them from Hitler's grasp and financed the rebuilding of their cities and industries through the Marshall Plan."

Emile looked intently into his cousin's troubled eyes. "But back to Nathan. What can we do to help?"

"I think," replied Gilmary, "he needs the guidance of a strong man." Then realizing how that might sound to her cousin, she added quickly, "Not that you aren't strong, Emile. You're amazingly strong and resourceful. But you're also too close to him in age. No, he needs an older person, someone experienced with adversity."

Emile smiled at her serious expression. "I think you're describing Peter MacAllister. We don't know any other really strong guy."

Gilmary frowned and bit her lip. "Strong he is, and he has the added advantage of being in the CIA. The problem's that he operates in Rome, and we aren't there. I don't even have a phone number or address for him. Arthur Leventhal knows his whereabouts, but my current contact with Arthur is through my mother, who's in Norway this week."

Emile's gaze swept over the other diners in the restaurant, stopping to rest on a middle-aged man at the next table, who held his fork and knife the American way. "Paris is known as the spy capital of Europe since NATO makes its home here. I'm sure there're CIA agents here too, maybe not in this bistro, but hidden deep within this European capital."

His cousin shook her head. "No, it's got to be Peter. He knows our situation." Suddenly Gilmary snapped her fingers. "I know it's a long shot, but maybe I can get word to Peter through his girlfriend."

"He has a girlfriend that he told you about?" Emile's expression was doubtful.

"Yes, and she's here in Paris." Instantly rummaging through her plain black purse, she triumphantly extracted a carefully folded piece of paper. She had pestered Peter enough to get an address from him before she left Rome in the fall.

"Rue des Rosiers, 13. Do you know where that is?"

Emile answered, "I've heard of it. It's somewhere in the Marais district near the Place St-Paul. Historically, it was called 'The Pletzl' and was at the center of the Jewish quarter. It's very crowded, partly because it's near to the Place des Vosges, one of the most popular places for the locals to relax."

"Well," said the young nun with finality, "It's the only lead we have so I'd better follow up on it."

Magnificent on this glorious Saturday morning, Paris sparkled in the sunlight. Thus Gilmary chose to ride a bus rather than the Paris Metro so she could enjoy people-watching as they traveled along the boulevards. Right now she had her nose plastered to the window as she craned her neck to get a better look at a tourist who was wobbly balancing on the parapet overlooking the bank of the Seine while trying to snap a photo of the back of Notre Dame Cathedral. But the driver of the #3 bus studiously ignored that scene. He had his hands full just dodging the tourists and shoppers cutting across his path as he crawled across the Ile Saint-Louis, known as the navel of Paris because of its location and history. Picking up speed as the bus reached the Pont de Sully he tried to make up time while crossing the river, but ended up lurching to a stop just before entering the Right Bank. Turning her face away from the window, Gilmary found a bag of baguettes dumped on her lap. Catching the eye of the frazzled woman next to her, she smiled as she returned the bag to the lady's overwhelmed arms.

The middle-aged woman, with short graying curls sticking out from under her beret, shook her head and spoke in French. "This driver's crazy! Too bad I can't afford a taxi. It would be better for my vegetables and baguettes. The vegetables will already be beaten into a puree before I even reach home."

The younger woman grinned. This bus ride reminded her of the buses in Rome. Only this was Paris, so the drivers were more respectful of the traffic rules, but not much more. In a way, though, Gilmary preferred Rome's street drama. It was unpredictable, just like life.

Upon stepping down from the bus, Gilmary strolled to Rue des Rosiers, 13. Stopping in front of an ancient apartment building, she faced an impressive wooden door ornamented with floral carvings. Frowning in concentration, Gilmary scanned the short list of tenants, looking for the name of Odette Millon. That was the name Peter had given her. But no, there was no Odette.

Shrugging her shoulders, Gilmary chose a random button to ring. After a couple of minutes, a pleasant, young voice responded, "Who is it?"

Leaning in towards the intercom, the nun explained. "This is Sister Gilmary. I'm an American friend of Peter MacAllister's and am looking for someone who can get in contact with him."

Before she knew it, she was buzzed in and standing at the open door of a dark-haired woman with smooth olive skin and sparkling hazel eyes. The woman's smile was more inquisitive than welcoming. Why was a young nun looking for Peter MacAllister here?

Gilmary held out her hand. "You must be Odette Millon. Peter spoke of you."

The young woman's smile turned into a snort as she laughed. Motioning the nun to enter her foyer, she tried to control her mirth, but failed. "What's this about Odette Millon?"

Looking confused, Gilmary said, "Peter told me he had a girlfriend in Paris named Odette Millon. Isn't that you?"

Breaking into chuckles again, the woman responded, "I'm a friend of Peter's, but not his current girlfriend and certainly not Odette Millon! My name's Iris Boyagian. Peter and I have worked together in the past, but not recently. But the Odette Millon thing—I think he was pulling your chain. Oops! I mean he was having fun deceiving you. He can be a great kidder."

Gilmary's embarrassment showed as she said, "Well, all kidding aside, I'm wondering if you can get hold of him for me. There's a family problem, and I think he can help us. Do you have a way of getting a message to him?"

Iris finally composed herself. "Yes, I can get word to him for you. Give me your name and how you can be reached, but I don't know how long it could take. You know, he might be difficult to find."

Later that day, when Gilmary was walking with Emile after they had visited Nathan at the jail and assured him of their help, she still fumed. "Crazy Peter! I haven't been so embarrassed in a long time. That woman, Iris, must think that I'm screwy!"

Emile was amused by his cousin's consternation. "What'd Peter do that has you in such a tizzy?"

"He told me his girlfriend, who, by the way, isn't his girlfriend, was living here and her name is Odette Millon."

"Odette Millon!" Emile now started to guffaw. It was too funny, and it showed how sheltered his nun cousin had been these last few years.

"Who's Odette?" asked his cousin.

Taking Gilmary by the elbow, Emile steered her to the nearby display window of a women's shoe store. Silently he pointed to a sophisticated arrangement of dressy pumps while he studied his cousin's expression. Above the shoes a sign was displayed reading, "*Odette Millon: Elegant Shoes designed for Comfort and Compliments*".

Gilmary's mouth dropped open as she began to understand Peter's deception. Rummaging through her memory, she recalled that she and Peter were standing on Via Faustina in Rome when he told her about his girlfriend. They had just returned from a tutorial on the motorcycle she'd have to drive. Because she couldn't ride it in her nun's habit while on the same cycle with Peter, she was dressed as a modest hippy, which fit right in with his disguise that day. An ancient Italian lady had come along the cobblestoned street, saw them and thought they were girlfriend and boyfriend. Gilmary felt embarrassed by that. She expected Peter would have a real girlfriend. After all, he was attractive, even if he was an elusive CIA agent in Rome.

Now she remembered that they'd been standing in front of a shoe store. She had her back to it, but he would have been facing it. No doubt there'd been a display of Odette Millon shoes. It wouldn't have interested her, since her sturdy nun's shoes were standard issue. All nuns wore the same style of black oxfords. She hadn't even looked at ladies' pumps for a few years. That rascal Peter! She'd rake him over the coals the next time she saw him.

Chapter Five

Rome

As the young woman stood looking into the shop window on Via dei Condotti in Rome's toniest shopping neighborhood, the sun warmed her back. It felt so comforting; something she had missed enormously while incarcerated in the prison in Sardinia.

Smiling contentedly, she focused on her reflection staring back at her. The new, honey-colored hue of her hair pleased her and garnered admiring glances from the Italian Lotharios passing by. *"Sei bellisima! Tu sei una stella, amore mio,"* she heard behind her. Italian men were attracted to blondes, and the hair color also made her feel more Teutonic.

Sighing and turning away from the display window, Olga returned to contemplating her predicament. On this bright Roman morning, her most pressing problem was money. The cash stolen from the German tourist had run out, so now she was floating a new idea. Her being in front of this particular store was no accident. Attractively displayed in the window were leather purses of various sizes, textures and hues. The current hot item was the dark-red "Volcano Collection". Two sizes of handbags completed the limited collection: the Etna, the larger of the two, and the smaller Vesuvius. Both were shaped wider at the base and narrower at the top clasp. Supposedly, they resembled volcanoes about to erupt when they were fully loaded with the stuff women carried with them everywhere. Olga thought the

32

marketing of them was ingenious. Already she saw women with the large and small volcanoes dangling from their arms sauntering among the other shoppers.

At present, she carried no purse, so she walked into the shop empty-handed and mingled with the enthusiastic crowd around a table of leather bags. A minute later, she emerged with an Etna that was large enough for her purposes. It had been easy to snatch among the many hands that plied the small mountain of purses.

Shielding her eyes from the sun, she peered down the street. Vitucci, a shop purveying very expensive jewelry, was attracting a wealthy clientele as usual. Tucking her honeyed hair into the floppy straw hat she had brought with her, she headed for the money.

After sizing up the crowd at the jewelry counters, Olga sidled up to a wealthy matron, who already displayed a small fortune of jewels on her fingers and wrists. A heavy pendant nestled in her ample décolletage. Best of all, the heavily-rouged woman had parked her red leather handbag on the countertop beside her. It also was an Etna. How convenient!

Smiling ingratiatingly at the store clerk, the rouged matron asked, "I just adore that diamond ring with the rubies surrounding it. What size is it? Could you take it out of the case so I can admire it better?"

As Olga approached, she placed her handbag immediately next to the lady's. The matron instinctively moved closer to her bag, but kept her eyes on the diamond ring that she was now admiring on her plump finger.

"*E bellisima, signora,*" purred the saleslady. Then she momentarily turned away to answer another customer's question.

Nodding in delightful agreement, the plump lady never noticed that her handbag had slid off the counter. Out of the corner of her eye, she still saw the red leather Etna next to her right arm.

As briskly as possible, Olga confidently raised her chin, straightened her back and gracefully exited the store. Fearing that her deception would be discovered as soon as the matron decided to purchase the ring, she tore off the straw hat that had covered her hair and threw it in the trash. Then she crossed the street and continued walking briskly for four blocks before stopping to order a cappuccino at a sidewalk café.

As the waiter returned with her order, he smiled. "Ah, signorina, you have the latest in handbags. So many of the ladies are carrying little volcanoes. It's all the rage, but a little amusing, don't you think?"

Olga laughed contentedly. She couldn't wait to open the bag and see how many lire it contained. Thousands upon thousands she hoped, since with inflation it took more than a thousand lire to buy a cappuccino.

Forty minutes later found her entering a familiar Roman neighborhood. Around the corner was the inconspicuous watch repair shop of Guiseppi Russo. A year ago, she had been in this communist sympathizer's establishment, so she knew he could do fine counterfeiting work. Today, though, she hoped he wouldn't recognize her since she had changed her hair and clothing style. She didn't want him to pass the word that she was back in circulation. She feared her handlers would send her back to East Berlin or the USSR in disgrace over the Aldo Falucci fiasco. She still burned inside when she thought of it. The despicable CIA had kidnapped her before she could act on that crucial job.

She expected the young nun she'd seen in the basilica the day she was kidnapped must have been set up to impersonate her and foil the plot. Even though she'd only seen her for a moment, she realized their resemblance was uncanny. She was truly her doppelganger.

Alone in the store, Guiseppi Russo looked up sharply as

the door opened and a young blonde woman entered humming the tune, *"Avanti o popolo"*. It was the sign that this was Communist Party business.

Checking to see if anyone else seemed interested enough to loiter outside the shop, and finding no one, he motioned the woman to follow him into the back room.

"Buona sera, signorina. How may I help you today? Do you need a watch repaired? Come back here where we can open it and see what's wrong."

"Of course, it needs repair since it has stopped working all together," said Olga quietly as she slid the stolen passport across the table to the counterfeiter.

Guiseppi examined the passport carefully. "Ah, I see you have a Margarethe. They are quite rare these days. I can repair it with parts from a Trudy Becker, if you wish. Do you want any other of its workings replaced? Also, I see it has a gear from Augsburg, and maybe we should change that to a Strasbourg gear. Their gears are far superior."

"You seem very good at diagnosing the problem. When can I expect to be able to claim the watch again?"

"No problem, signorina. These repairs can be done in a day. Come back tomorrow at this time. It will be ready," he said with a broad wink.

Chapter Six

Luxembourg City
May 5, 1965

A spring day in Luxembourg can be fickle. One moment a caressing softness envelops the countryside; then the wind shifts and a cool dampness creeps in from the Atlantic. But today was perfect, so all of Luxembourg City was out lining the streets near the cathedral to cheer on the May Springtime parade. Every marching band from the provinces was enthusiastically cheered as much as the local city bands. The Luxembourgers were proud of all of them.

Gilmary thought fondly of the parades back home where the Scottish and Irish bagpipers marched. Well, there wouldn't be bagpipers here, but there were spritely stepping dancers preceding some of the bands.

Standing to her left were Emile and Nathan, who had been allowed to come home until his trial. The Parisian police had made Gilmary swear that she would bring him back later this spring in time for his court appearance in Paris. On her right, with her feet tapping in time to the beat of the drums and her hands energetically waving small Luxembourger flags stood Sister Maria Goretti.

Laughing, with her dimples on display, Maria Goretti turned to her friend Gilmary. "How I love parades! I only wish I could join those dancers. Of course, if I did, Mother Assumpta wouldn't approve. And think of Sister Tomasina! She already thinks we're depraved and a disgrace to the community."

Gilmary winked conspiratorially. "Come next week, we could dance in the street and no one would bat an eyelid."

"You're right," agreed Maria Goretti bobbing her head and turning back to the parade.

The previous Thursday, when Maria Goretti had arrived at the von Hollenden home from Wisconsin, she unpacked a surprise for her friend and classmate, Gilmary. It was a woman's navy blue suit with a short veil. Because of the modernizing changes flowing from the Vatican II meetings in Rome, many nuns were experimenting with wearing a modified habit. Their community in Racine had decided to retire their long, medieval white garb for a modest suit and modified veil. For several of the women's religious orders, it was just one of the more radical steps towards entering a new age.

Standing on the curb across the way was a handsome, blond man in his early thirties. His gaze had scanned the happy crowd and come to rest on the little group surrounding the two nuns across from him. Breaking into a grin, his spirits were lifted when he saw his old friends. There were Gilmary, Emile, Maria Goretti and another young man who bore a striking resemblance to Gilmary. He surmised the boy was her brother. The expressive, arched brows were the same, even though the boy had lighter hair than his sister's auburn locks. He remembered her reddish hair from the two times they had practiced riding the motorcycle together in Rome.

Behind him a small boy suddenly ran into him, and the force of the collision made the child lose control of the balloon he held. He wailed loudly, and Peter MacAllister, the young blond man, jumped up to grab the balloon, returning it to the teartul boy. When Peter turned again towards the parade, something sharp hit him smack in the forehead. Stunned, he looked up and saw Emile and the little group around him laughing and waving manically at him.

Just moments before, Emile had spied Peter in the crowd. Grabbing a flyer advertising sight-seeing tours that someone had just given him, he fashioned a paper airplane and aimed it squarely at the CIA agent. Bingo! A direct hit!

A couple of hours later, Peter and the reunited group were sitting around a cozy fire in the von Hollenden living room. Nathan was sitting across from the CIA agent, who was nonchalantly removing a briar pipe from his pocket, and the boy couldn't take his eyes off him. Here was a real spy! Even though he worked for imperialistic America, he was fascinating.

Of course, it wasn't told to Nathan that Peter was a spy. No, he'd overheard a private conversation between his sister and Emile when they were discussing Peter's arrival. But there were still secrets he wasn't aware of. Little did Nathan know that his sister, whom he called Philomena or Phil, which was her name in the family, had impersonated a Stasi assassin just last summer in Rome in order to foil a Soviet plot. The little group around the fire hadn't even mentioned it. Even better, he didn't know that his mother had been recruited to help the CIA. Such information would have confused the young man's Maoist-influenced mind.

Tapping the Virginia tobacco into the bowl of his pipe, Peter winked at Gilmary, who noticed how mesmerized Nathan seemed to be by the agent.

"Emile, are you a baseball fan? I imagine you'd have gone to a few games as a teenager living in America."

Emile, who was curled up closest to the fireplace with his knees folded up to his chin, made a face. "You usually don't get to see professional teams like the Milwaukee Braves when you're living on a farm in the middle of the Iowa cornfields—but you're right. Baseball's a favorite pastime for everyone in the little prairie towns. What else could you do on a Friday or Saturday night, except go and cheer on the local team?"

Nathan perked up as he recollected the fun of chasing with his friends around the bleachers at those community games. "I remember cheering for Emile, who was usually in the outfield. His throwing was just so-so, but he sure could run fast."

"The only problem was I couldn't hit well, so my chances for running and scoring were almost nil," Emile offered with a sheepish grin.

"Well," continued Peter, "as I was growing up in Ann Arbor, Michigan, my favorite team was the nearby Detroit Tigers. My dad, older brother, Reggie, and I would try to see half dozen home games each season. What fascinated me were the hand signals that the pitcher, batters and coaches used so they could secretly communicate with each other."

As if to demonstrate, Peter touched his right ear lobe, then his left lobe and finally pretended to adjust his non-existent baseball cap.

Maria Goretti cocked her head and looked quizzically at him. "What's that mean?"

Peter laughed. "It means whatever we've agreed upon before the game. Maybe we said that in the first inning it would mean bunt the ball or steal a base."

She was still perplexed. "Then what would it mean during the second inning?"

Peter waved his pipe in the air. "Oh, again whatever we'd agreed on in the dugout between innings that we would use for that second inning. Trying to remember the various meanings and non-meanings of the signs stretches your memory."

"You're making baseball almost sound cerebral," Gilmary chuckled.

"I'll tell you what," said Emile, "let's make up some signs and see if we can guess what they mean. Maria Goretti, you go first. Give us a signal."

The young nun, who was seated on the carpet on the other side of the fireplace, touched her left shoulder with her right hand, then ran her hand to her right earlobe and finally touched the tip of her nose.

"I know," offered Nathan enthusiastically. "You're telling the player on second base to run to third and continue home on the next hit. Am I right?"

Maria Goretti laughed merrily. "That's as good a guess as any. Since I don't know much about baseball, I can't think up really good scenarios."

Emile jumped up and got everyone's attention. "Watch this!" he said as he massaged his bristly chin twice, ran his hand up to his nose and ended at the brim of his imaginary cap.

"You're the third base coach, and you want the batter to bunt the ball while the guy on first steals second," Nathan said with confidence.

"That's close. I am the third base coach and I do want the batter to bunt all right."

While Peter tapped out his pipe, he looked at the group around the fireplace and smiled. "I think you're getting good at this. Let's play a game of baseball later this evening and try out our signals."

But Nathan had his doubts. "It won't be much of a game with only five of us, but I'll get my pal, Fabian, to join us so at least we have enough people for all of the bases. Then we can take turns at the bat and make our silly signals."

Chapter Seven

The next day, Peter suggested he and Gilmary take a solitary walk along the Petrusse River. The sense of exclusion at not being asked to accompany them bruised Maria Goretti and Nathan's feelings, but Emile offered instead to drive them on a tour of the spring countryside and on to Echtennach on the Mosel River, where he would treat them to lunch.

Gilmary, thrilled that Peter was interested in a city which meant a lot to her, proudly led him to view the Petrusse River valley, a dramatic scene glimpsed at the bottom of a deep gorge that cleaved the capital city of Luxembourg into two parts. On one side of the modest stream, there was a formidable wall of stone, pierced intermittently by man-made caverns. The immense size of the monolithic granite facade dwarfed the river running beside it. Standing on the pathway below and next to the sparkling river, Peter asked, "Tell me about those crude and mysterious openings in the wall."

Gilmary responded, "They do look mysterious, but they weren't always so crude-looking. Each of those large holes is meant to house cannon, and at one time they did. Behind the holes there's a labyrinth of tunnels that originally extended fourteen miles. However, several miles of the tunnels have been blocked since the late 1800s."

Peter shielded his eyes from the sun as he scanned the steep cliff before them. "What an engineering marvel! Are the tunnels open to the public?"

"Yes, there're tours of a section of it. In fact a friend of our family, who's a teacher during the week, is a tour guide on weekends and holidays. Her name is Tilly, and we can join her for a tour tomorrow, if you'd like."

After that, Peter seemed preoccupied as they wandered through the town and back along Rue Jacques Parmentier towards the oldest section of the city. As they approached a small square, where a fountain playing in the sunlight was the focal point, Peter motioned Gilmary towards a table in the shade under a blue awning outside a corner café.

"What would you like to drink?"

"I'll have whatever you're having," replied Gilmary equably.

"Well, after our hike, I'd like a beer," Then Peter leaned back in his chair and wiped his brow. He had developed a taste for one of the strong-bodied Belgian beers while he was living in Paris and in training for NATO. Since then he always drank Westmalle Dubbel if he could find it.

When the waiter had brought them each a glass of the foamy, brown beer, Peter eyed the nun dubiously. Would she really like a dark beer? Wasn't tea more to her taste?

Winking at him and raising her glass, Gilmary toasted. "To the Belgian monks, who denied themselves a lot but rewarded themselves and us with the pleasure of a fine beverage!"

After a couple of moments spent enjoying their rest and refreshment, Gilmary turned a critical eye on Peter. "Odette Millon," she said simply.

Peter looked up suddenly and tried to gauge her meaning. A small prick of his conscience and her tone of voice made him apprehensive. He tried to put on his most innocent look, but Gilmary wasn't buying it. After all, she'd seen her brother and Emile try the same look when they were as guilty as hell.

Quickly she explained how she had tracked him down

through Iris Boyagian in Paris. He already knew that Iris was the one who had sent word to him in Rome via Arthur Leventhal.

"Why'd you tell me about Odette Millon and play me for a fool?" Gilmary said with irritation as she recalled her embarrassment when Iris had laughed at her.

Peter cleared his throat while stalling for time. "You'll remember that we'd just returned from our motorcycle riding practice along the Tiber when an old lady approached us and thought we were romantically attached. I could see that what she said bothered you, so I guess I said something dumb. I figured that if you thought I had a girlfriend it would take some of the embarrassment out of the situation. I didn't want you to be uncomfortable since we had to work together. You know…I wanted to keep it professional."

"But why Odette Millon—a shoe of all things?"

"It's the best I could come up with on the spur of the moment. And it was French, so you wouldn't come across such a girl in Rome. Really, believe me. I didn't do it to make fun of you. I'd never do that. Actually, I've tremendous respect for your spunk. I'm still in awe of how you were able to pull off the impersonation of Olga, the Stasi assassin, and then survive your imprisonment in the villa in Florence."

Gilmary tried to quiet her conflicting emotions. On one hand she was still hurt and angry, but on the other she could appreciate that Peter had lied to her to save her feelings.

Peter reached across the small table to shake hands. "I'm really sorry I embarrassed you. I was trying to save us embarrassment, but it backfired. Can we be friends?"

Gilmary shook Peter's hand and smiled. "Of course we're friends. After all, I asked you to come and help us out with my little brother. Do you have any ideas of how to straighten things out?"

"I do, but first I'll have to run my idea past Arthur in Rome. He's my boss, and also his influence can probably get

Nathan out of having to go to trial in France. I'm leaving for Rome on Monday morning's train. I hope to return in a few days with a plan. Until then you can keep Nathan busy and out of trouble. He's really a good kid—and not so much of a kid anymore at eighteen. He just needs someone to point him in the right direction and he'll fly on his own."

"It's hard for us to imagine what this would have looked like one hundred and seventy-one years ago when the French were besieging our people in 1794." Tilly, the tour guide of the Casements labyrinth of tunnels, was warming to her subject. It was a good crowd that stood attentively before her. Even the clique of teenagers, staying as far away from their parents as allowed, seemed interested.

"The several thousand people from the city above us, as well as the folks from the surrounding countryside, had to cooperate in these narrow confines to survive for the seven months of the siege. Here they even had bakeries and kitchens as well as workshops and stables. Over there in that dark corner, was the forty-seven meter deep well that provided all their water."

Gilmary was pleased Peter seemed truly interested in the tour of the Casements, with their impressive length and depth. She remembered how awed she felt the first time her mother brought her here with Nathan. Her mother wanted them to know and be proud of their Luxembourgish heritage.

Tilly was motioning everyone to follow her into the next cavern. She stopped then and stood in the light of one of the large openings which overlooked the Petrusse River, a dizzying twenty-seven meters below.

"During World War II, our little country of three hundred thousand people was overrun on the 10th of May, 1940 by the formidable army of the Third Reich. We'd been declared a neutral country by the Second Treaty of London in 1867, but, as we know, neutrality meant nothing to Adolph Hitler.

"During the bombardments that followed, these caverns were our shelter. The labyrinth of tunnels could hold thirty-five thousand brave, but frightened people. For five years, we suffered grievously under the German occupation. Sadly, many of our young men at that time were forcibly sent by the Nazis to the eastern front of the war towards Russia. They weren't given clothing and supplies necessary to fight in the harsh winter weather, and sometimes they weren't even given weapons. Basically, they were cannon fodder. Some of our boys, however, were able to escape our country and go to England. There they joined the Allies and helped in our liberation. Nevertheless, that's why there are fewer men of forty years here than would be expected. A lot of that generation was wiped out by the war.

"Those of us who lived through the occupation and the subsequent liberation are eternally grateful to the Americans and British, as well as others who helped to liberate us. Also, before you leave our country, be sure to visit the American Cemetery, where there are the graves of those valiant soldiers who died here. You'll find it sobering to see the scale of the cemetery. You'll also be proud of the bravery of those men."

After ending the tour, Gilmary and Peter stood pensively on the Place de la Constitution, overlooking the river. Now they could envision the warren of tunnels hidden beneath their feet. As a sudden cool wind whipped up from the valley below, Peter turned and said, "That tour was instructive. And if you didn't know the history of those Casemates, you'd never guess what lies beneath our feet. I wonder if Arthur knows about them?"

Gilmary smiled archly. "Arthur gives the impression of knowing everything, so I'd guess he filed this info someplace in his mental encyclopedia."

Chapter Eight

Rome

Wednesday morning Peter awoke in his own bed and to the familiar noises of the Trastevere neighborhood in Rome. Luxembourg City had been so much quieter and cooler. Here the sun from the east and the warm breezes from the west sneaked through his balcony window and warmed the apartment. They were both welcome, he thought, as he stretched and prepared to shower.

This morning he had an appointment with Arthur Leventhal, his CIA boss. He knew Arthur was tasked with arming the "stay-behind" armies of the free European nations. It was a top priority of NATO and a tremendous responsibility.

An hour later, as Peter sat across the desk from the Rome CIA chief, he felt like pulling out his pipe, since smoking helped him think. But he regretfully thought better of it while sitting here with Arthur, whose only stimulant was coffee. Instead, Peter took another sip from his cup.

Leventhal had explained how he had enlisted Madame von Hollenden to find agents in free countries who could expedite the flow of new hidden weapons for their clandestine armies.

"She has the perfect cover for the job with her rose society work. Who would suspect such a graceful and cultured lady of being an agent? I certainly wouldn't if I hadn't recruited her myself." He said this with a certain amount of satisfaction.

Peter looked at his boss with less satisfaction. Arthur had

just shocked him with a new scheme that would involve Gilmary in a dangerous ruse of deception. "Madame von Hollenden's job carries less risk, I think, than the job you want her daughter to do for us. Gilmary will have to meet face-to-face with a Soviet agent and believably deceive him. If the agent doesn't accept her story, her life will probably be jeopardized. Do you really want to put her in such a precarious position?"

Arthur played with the pencil on his desk, first making a circle on the blotter with the eraser and then turning it onto its tip. "I live with a perpetually guilty conscience, Peter. Certainly I don't want to involve untrained citizens in this espionage work. But sometimes they're in a position that the Commies find trustworthy and innocent enough. It would take a long time to put one of our agents in place in order to believably pull off this deception.

"Besides, Gilmary or Philomena, the name I knew her by as a child, has already been accepted as a Soviet spy by the communists here in Italy. If they still believe she was arrested by the Italian carabinieri and then escaped, they'll probably accept her as Olga Diederich in Luxembourg. The trick is to put her in touch with an influential communist agent in Luxembourg City."

"What about the real Olga Diederich? I hope she's still in the Capo Marrargui prison in Sardinia. I heard a rumor about a riot inside the prison there. Did anyone escape?"

Arthur wished the subject of the prison riot had not been broached. "Three prisoners escaped during the riot. Two were Russians and the third was the East German agent, Olga Diederich. The two Russians never got off of the beach. Olga did and disappeared into the island. However, a canoe that was stolen from the marina at the fishing village of Dosa turned up floating empty just off the western coast a few miles north of the prison. We think Olga paddled the canoe into the open waters of the Mediterranean and capsized, although her body has never been found."

Abruptly, Arthur stopped telling the story there. He did not continue with the account of the young German teacher on holiday in Sardinia, who told of being tied up and robbed in the Grotto di Netunno. That was an unsolved case. It did involve a young woman perpetrator, however, so it left open the possibility that Olga was on the loose. Arthur fervently hoped that was not the reality.

Chapter Nine

"Luxembourg City! This is Luxembourg City. Exit towards the right, please. The announcement was made crisply in French, German and Luxembourg by the wiry and efficient conductor, traveling through the cars, doing his best to alert most of the passengers in their own language.

Olga stared intently out of the grimy window of the decelerating train. They were entering the city, and she was curious to see a place that she had only heard about. Some had called it the "Gibraltar of the North" because of its strategic position and the Casemates. Those Casemates she knew were the miles-long tunneled network of caverns honeycombing the south side of the chasm that cleaved the city in two. Since the army that held the city's fortifications also held the line of defense, armies had fought for centuries over their ownership. Other than that tidbit of history, she knew little about the small duchy, but it appeared very clean and attractive.

Of course, she wasn't here as a tourist. No, if tourism were her objective, she'd be in the Balearic Islands encamped on a beach. Unexpectedly, a chance encounter in Rome had pointed her north like a bloodhound sniffing out its prey.

She recollected that it was midday on a Thursday and just after one o'clock—lunch and siesta time; the usual time for the shopkeepers to pull down the metal doors that protected their stores when they were closed. Outside of a fruit stall on Via Napoleone III, in a poor neighborhood of Rome, a tired-looking woman was moving a crate of oranges into her shop. Olga, who was mentally practicing details of her new passport identity, didn't see the woman until she knocked into her and set the oranges rolling.

"*O mi scusi, signora.* I was distracted," apologized Olga. Crouching to retrieve some of the fruit, she then rose and finally looked into the woman's tired eyes.

"Rosa!" exclaimed Olga. "I thought you were in Firenze. What are you doing here? I would never have expected to see you in Rome."

The woman, holding the fruit in her apron, peered quizzically at Olga, not recognizing her, but suspicious because this stranger knew she had last lived in Firenze.

"Oh Rosa, of course you don't recognize me." Then Olga made a quick decision. She would confide in this woman, whom she had met in Firenze at a meeting in a communist safe house. It had been more than a year ago, and the meeting had only lasted two hours, but she might know more of what had happened in the Aldo Falucci affair and the whereabouts of the young nun, her doppelganger.

Leading the way through the aisle of crates of fruit and back into the store, Olga hummed *"Avanti o popolo"* loud enough for the woman to hear.

Quickly Rosa lowered the corrugated metal door and sought the dim back room where Olga had already made herself comfortable.

Smiling conspiratorially, Olga motioned the wary woman to sit. "Do you have a little white wine, Rosa? I'm thirsty from walking." Actually, the assassin wanted Rosa to relax. Especially she wanted her tongue to relax so Olga could pump her for information.

A few minutes later, when the wine had begun to mellow

the mood, Olga began her interrogation.

"Rosa, I'm Olga Diederich, East German, and a trained Stasi assassin, working for the Soviets. You may have heard of the successful assassination of a journalist here in Rome last April. That was my contribution to the communist cause."

The tired shopkeeper sat up more alert now. She did remember meeting this young woman, only today she looked different—blonde, chic in her dress and more polished. Looking down at the woman's well-clad feet, she felt a pang of jealousy as she perused the other's Odette Millon high heels. It was rare for Rosa to indulge herself. She had two children to support on her own, and the Communist Party was unreliable in its monetary allowance.

Olga continued, "You'd have read in July of a successful poisoning of Aldo Falucci, if I'd still been able to ply my trade. Unfortunately, I was captured by the CIA and imprisoned in Sardinia."

Rosa interrupted, "Olga Diederich! You do look quite different. Still, I'm so confused. You stayed with us in Firenze just months ago. Weren't you arrested by the Italian carabinieri at the villa near the Piazzale Michelangolo?"

"No, that wasn't me, but a look-alike the CIA must have inserted in my place. She was the one who failed to kill Signore Falucci. She wasn't supposed to kill him—only make it look real. I doubt if she really was arrested by the carabinieri. Her arrest was probably a ruse." The thought of it made Olga become visibly agitated.

Rosa paused a moment before saying, "Well, if it was a ruse, it came just in time for her because that evening she was supposed to be moved back behind the Western Bloc and into East Berlin. It was because of the raid that we had to abandon the safe house and scatter."

Olga stared intently into Rosa's eyes. "Do you have any idea where she came from or where she went?"

"No, not really anything concrete since we all believed her to be you. She spoke German, although I cannot say if she had an accent. Her voice was softer and a little higher than yours. She was gentler, and the children loved to play games with her." This description of the other Olga, the one she had come to like in Firenze, made her suddenly dislike this comrade in the room with her.

Olga sensed the subtle change in mood and knew she had to manipulate the woman carefully. "Do you think she may have been a real nun?"

"She may have been. I searched her room one day and found a religious dress carefully hung in her closet. Also, there were notes, maybe poems or prayers written on scraps of paper. They weren't in Italian or in German, which I can't read or speak, but I know what it looks like. Instead they were in a language a little like German."

Now Olga felt she had some clues she could use to help her understand her antagonist. Her doppelganger was probably a true, young Dominican nun, who spoke German and Italian and some other Germanic language which was probably her native tongue. Could it be Dutch? Or even Luxembourg? The Luxembourgers were more likely to be Catholic and devout. Also, the woman probably spoke Russian, since otherwise the Russian agents at the safe house would have found her suspect. That was certainly an admirable catalogue of languages. No wonder the CIA used her as a spy.

Rosa got up from her chair and removed the bottle of wine from the table. "You'll have to go now. It's the siesta hour, and my children will be here soon. I wish you well."

Olga's eyes narrowed. She didn't like to have the older woman close the conversation. Nevertheless, Rosa's mention of her children gave her an idea. She badly needed for this woman to keep her whereabouts secret.

"Rosa, no one must know you've seen me and told me

these things. I think you understand why."

The other woman nodded slowly in assent. This Stasi agent would be in deep trouble if her handlers called her to account for why she had been caught by the CIA. Their plan to kill the president of the Christian Democratic Party, a great unifier, and then insert their own secret communist as the new president, completely fell apart when Aldo Falucci survived the attempt on his life. Also Silvio Bertollini, the communist mole they intended to substitute as the new president of the party, had been arrested and not seen since then.

Presently, from the street there was a light pounding on the metal door. Both woman broke their gaze and turned towards the front of the shop. Rosa's children had arrived home from school, for the family lived above the store.

Grabbing Rosa by her neck and one wrist, Olga's face suddenly became ugly. "I know you love your children. I would too if I were their mother. But I'm not. I'm an assassin, and I punish those who don't keep secrets!"

Rosa was shocked by the change in Olga's tone and appearance. The young woman's grip was like a steel manacle. Wide-eyed, she looked up at Olga and nodded her understanding. Then without another look, Olga loosened her steely grip, dropped her arms and strode quickly to the front of the store.

Surprised at seeing someone leave the shuttered store at siesta, the children stepped back to let her pass. Abruptly, Olga turned and intently scrutinized first the girl's face and then the little boy's. Finally she turned and gave a hard, knowing last look at Rosa, who blanched at the other woman's piercing stare.

Chapter Ten

Luxembourg City

Peter was as good as his word, for he returned the following Monday with surprising news. He had seen Arthur in Rome and had gotten his help in voiding Nathan's arrest in Paris. Gilmary was stunned by the good news and marveled at Arthur's clout with the French justice system.

Madam von Hollenden was still doing business in Sweden, and Emile had returned to his cooking school in France, but Nathan, Gilmary, and Maria Goretti were home in Luxembourg City and received the news ecstatically.

"I have a plan, Nathan," Peter offered as they all sat together in the von Hollenden study. "How'd you like to attend the University of Michigan next semester? It's a top-notch school,—better than the place you were at—and you could live with my brother Reggie's family. My parents still live there too, so there'd be lots of family for you, and lots of baseball too."

Nathan looked surprised. He knew he'd burned his bridges in Paris. The university had kicked him and his buddies out for good. He didn't have a back-up plan and feared facing his mother when she returned. The more he considered Peter's idea, the more he liked it. Luxembourg seemed too small of a country for him. Also, he preferred speaking English. And baseball! Detroit Tiger games!

Gilmary and Maria Goretti, who were not sure how

Nathan would take Peter's offer, sighed in relief when Nathan showed enthusiasm for the idea. Gilmary rose and hugged her brother, while over his shoulder she smiled approvingly at Peter. Here was a man worth a thousand of other guys his age, she decided.

Peter then came over to Nathan, gave him a manly hug and slapped him heartedly on the back. When the boy stepped back, he straightened his shoulders and seemed a couple of inches taller. All six feet of him seemed stronger and lighter. He had a future now, while only moments ago he had felt caught in an uncertain limbo.

Later that afternoon when the rest of the house was quiet, Peter led Gilmary out to the veranda. After Gilmary had expressed again her gratitude for his efforts on behalf of her brother, she noticed how quiet the agent had become. Taking his time, Peter tapped the ash out of his pipe, carefully packed in fresh tobacco and began the process of lighting it. He was stalling for time as he decided how to lay out Arthur's plan involving the young nun.

When he had met with Leventhal in Rome a few days ago, Arthur had laid out a new plan for deceiving the Soviet agents in Luxembourg, and he badly wanted Gilmary's participation. He hoped the Soviets would still accept the young woman as a disguised, East German Stasi assassin in their employ.

Finally Peter got the pipe smoking to his liking and turned his attention to the patient nun. "Arthur needs your help," he started without preamble. "A new stash of weapons for the 'stay-behind' army will be delivered here soon. Of course, the Soviets want to know where they'll be hidden. They'd pay dearly for that information so they could be the first to uncover and use them in the event that they'd actually try to take over this country.

"Our best defense of that information is a good offense. We want to offer them some very believable misinformation."

Peter paused, and after a moment continued. "That's where you come into the picture. We want you to find a Soviet contact here. After he accepts you as another Soviet agent, you can give him the coveted information of where NATO has hidden the weapons cache." Peter's eyes narrowed as he looked at the nun and tried to gauge her reaction.

After her initial shock, Gilmary looked seriously at the agent. "You wouldn't want me to tell them the real information though. Won't the agents know almost immediately that what I tell them is bogus? All they'd have to do is look."

Peter smiled and drew on his pipe. "That wouldn't be much of a deception now, would it? And it would be the end of you. No, that's not how we'll do it. The hiding place of the real cache will be unknown even to you, so there's no way that you could accidently reveal it."

Gilmary grimaced. "Yes, but I may still hang by my thumbs while they try to find out that which I don't know."

Peter solemnly replied. "I don't think that will happen. You see, the tour of the Petrusse Casemates was very instructive, and also inspiring, I might add. Even a Soviet agent's imagination could conjure up the image of hidden armaments in those caves, so that's just what we'll do."

"You'll hide the armaments in the Casemates? I know there are miles of tunnels, but no matter what caverns you choose, they'll eventually find the stash."

"You're quite right," replied Peter. "And you are going to be the person to lead them to it."

Gilmary was confused but intelligent enough to wait for the whole explanation. Peter appreciated her calm. She didn't sputter or argue, so he continued.

"Ninety-five percent of our weapons will be stored at other sites around the countryside. One place in particular will have a majority of the weapons. Five percent, however, will actually be stored here in the Casements so it appears that all of it's here. The tourists only have access to a mile or more of the eleven miles of tunnels that still exist. The other three miles of the original tunnel length were destroyed long ago. At the end of the tour access, the labyrinth has been blocked off even though there are still tunnels beyond. Behind the blocked wall, we'll stockpile guns, ammunition, howitzers, hand grenades and lots of heavy crates in the first three caverns. Beyond that point every opening will be sealed, but you'll intimate that there's at least a quarter of a mile more of caverns full of armaments. If they doubt you, they can open crates in the first three caverns and find that every one of them contains guns or ammo."

Now Gilmary was beginning to understand the plan. "But how am I to find a Soviet agent here in Luxembourg City?"

"Arthur has a plan for that too. He doesn't leave much to chance. As you know, many foreigners come north looking for jobs. Most of the ones here immigrate from Italy or Portugal. Still, a few also manage to come from Poland and East Germany. Because they're usually only able to communicate in their native language, especially as far as writing, they need help reading documents or writing letters in French, Luxembourgish or German. That's where you come in."

Gilmary knew this first hand, as an Italian man, who helped prepare their flower beds in the spring and fall, sometimes asked her mother to translate a document or letter for him.

Peter waited to get her attention again. "In cities where migrants converge, there are scribes who are paid a nominal sum to translate or write for these folks. You may have seen them at desks near the city hall."

"I know they exist, but I've never paid much attention to them," said Gilmary.

"We want you and a companion to act as scribes so as to collect information from some of these temporary workers. Sooner or later, we think you'll get a lead on a Soviet agent because the Soviets are actively recruiting foreigners to join the

Communist Party."

Gilmary decided Arthur had hit upon a good plan in order to find a communist agent. "Sister Maria Goretti is here for the next couple of months as my companion. She has a working knowledge of Polish. I, of course, lived in Italy and majored in Russian and German in college, so we can cover at least four languages—five with English. Naturally I speak French and Luxembourgish too since I lived here a while, and my mother made sure that Nathan and I have a working knowledge of our native languages."

"For our purposes, we couldn't have found anyone better who has a facility in languages. What do you think? Will you be a part of this plan?"

Gilmary touched her eyes, ears and made a zipping motion across her mouth.

"What's that a signal for?" asked Peter.

"It means I'm the eyes and ears here for you and Arthur, and I'll keep my mouth shut!"

Feeling relieved, Peter laughed. "I guess those signs are pretty obvious."

Two days later, Madame von Hollenden returned home feeling flushed with success. She had located half dozen rose plants to repatriate to local gardens and made appropriate contacts in both countries concerning the secret weapons caches. She hoped her success was not just beginner's luck.

Peter was still there in Luxembourg City. He had waited to explain his plans for Nathan with his mother. If she didn't approve of the plan, he would have to make an alternative one. Just what it would be, he couldn't guess.

He needn't have worried, however, because Genevieve couldn't have been happier. The offer of Peter's family was beyond generous. It might prove a lifesaver for Nathan, or so she hoped.

Of course, she'd been mortified to learn that Nathan had become involved with petty crime and the political campus propaganda of Maoism. On top of that, to be arrested and expelled from the university! Still, on further thought, she was glad he'd been arrested. It alerted them all to the troubled path he'd been embarking upon.

Chapter Eleven

Meanwhile Maria Goretti and Gilmary were making the transition from their white habits and granny oxfords to new navy blue suits and low-heeled pumps.

"I actually like those old granny oxfords for walking on these cobblestones," remarked Maria Goretti as she caught her heel between a pair of cobbles. "And I feel self-conscious in these new clothes."

"We'll get used to them soon," Gilmary said confidently as she forged ahead towards the office that advertised the solicitor services of Weicker and Franck.

As they entered the doors to the anteroom, they waved to the secretary who sat behind a desk in the glassed-in offices of the two solicitors. The two scribes had their desks in the outer anteroom. Each had a glass-partitioned cubicle containing an ample desk, three chairs and a bookcase.

Maria Goretti sat down and tried out the swivel chair behind the oak desk in her glass cubical. Feeling excited and nervous, she checked her supplies. Yes, they were all there—typewriter, paper, carbon paper, pens, ink and blotters, pencils, erasers, stapler and a Polish/English dictionary. For some reason the word "*truskawka*" kept running like a tape recorder through her brain. "*Truskawka*" meant strawberry. Why was the only Polish word rattling around in her head "*truskawka*"?

Glancing sideways, she observed Gilmary lining up her dictionaries in a bookcase behind her desk. It then occurred to

Maria Goretti that her main purpose for being here was to be a companion to the other nun. After all, besides Polish and English, what did she know of languages? "*Nic!*"

Looking out the office windows at the street scene before them, Maria Goretti noticed how purposeful everyone seemed. The neatly dressed men and women moved along as if they knew the value of time. Even if the Luxembourgers did not like being compared to the Germans, who had occupied their country twice in the last half century, they appeared more like them than the more laid-back French. Nevertheless, French was the language one heard the most on the street after their native tongue. The Luxembourger patois was not recognized for official business. Instead knowledge of French was "*de rigeur*", except for police matters, where German was preferred.

Presently she focused on a middle-aged man in overalls and wearing a cloth cap, whose front brim shielded his forehead. He was cupping both hands around his eyes and squinting as he peered into their office from outside. Seeing the signs above their cubicles, he proceeded towards the door and entered.

Scrutinizing the signs more closely once inside, he moved past Gilmary and on to Maria Goretti. Removing his cap, he hesitated. Now that he was only a few feet from her, Maria Goretti noticed the white plaster that stuck in blotches to his overalls. He was a laborer—probably a lather.

After she motioned him to one of the chairs facing her, she could see the myriad of fine wrinkles that surrounded his eyes—kindly eyes. Why, he reminded her of her father!

Florian was her father's name. Back in Milwaukee in his gregarious way, he held court in his barber shop near the corner of Locust and Oakland Avenues. Just like this man, he had kindly blue eyes, surrounded by a cris-crossed map of wrinkles.

Feeling more confident now, Maria Goretti greeted the man in Polish, "*Dzien dobry.*" He responded, and smiling, pointed to the short veil on her head. "*Siostra?*" he asked.

"*Tok*," she replied.

He nodded in satisfaction, for even though she looked like a young girl, she must be well-educated and trustworthy.

Drawing a sheaf of papers out of an envelope, he smoothed and laid them before her. After ascertaining from him that it was a lease for an apartment he and three other Poles rented, she heard him describe the problem. One of the men was returning to Warsaw, their hometown. But Krzysztof, as this man was called, was afraid the lease would be voided if less than four people occupied the apartment. He thought the rent was set for each man separately, so now the owner would feel he was going to lose money and, as a result, would throw them out. Would she read the lease and see if there was a solution?

Looking down at the papers written in French, Maria Goretti realized her college French was not up to the job of translating technical legalese. With a sigh, she motioned Krzysztof to follow her to Gilmary's cubical.

A half hour later, the situation was clear. There was no escape clause; Krzysztof would have to find another man to fill the vacancy in their apartment. Rising from his chair, he looked slightly worried as he folded the lease and returned it to its envelope. "Tomorrow I'll go the migrant employment office and see what I can do." Then he bade them farewell.

Chapter Twelve

Dieter Braun was a quiet man; he was more given to listening and observing than speaking. No one was sure of his opinions and he preferred it that way. You see, Herr Braun was a Soviet spy.

He did not actually choose to collude with the Soviets. During World War II, he quietly but eagerly collaborated with the Nazis, who overran his so-called neutral country. Like the German invaders, he considered the little country of Luxembourg as an off-shoot of the German state. Surely, the Luxembourger language was more of a German dialect than the standardized language of Bonn and Berlin. But wasn't Alsatian as distinct from German grammar as the Luxembourger tongue? Everyone knew that Alsatian was German. Who here cared if a sausage was called a "*mustripen*" or a "*weisswurst*"; you ate it with horseradish regardless.

Anyway, after the Allies won the war and the Nuremburg trials tried to mete out justice as they saw it, Dieter kept his head down, expressed no opinion and started a rose garden. Roses did not question his allegiance, and they rewarded his tender attentions with blooms.

During the day, he was a gray suit, who dutifully opened the doors of the Freistadt Bank at precisely half past eight. Inevitably, the first customer at his cashier's cage was Frau Kolnberger, who added exactly eight francs a day to her account, except on Fridays, when she withdrew twenty francs. The money came from what her boarders paid for dinner each work day, but the news she brought to Herr Braun came from the Italian boarders and the shopkeepers from whom she bought her food stuffs daily. If there were other customers who were queuing up to do banking with Herr Braun, she would just run her gloved forefinger across her upper lip. That was interpreted by Dieter as an invitation to share a cup of coffee at one o'clock when he closed the bank for lunch.

Like Herr Braun, Frau Kolnberger was not a willing Soviet comrade. She too had collaborated with the German Wehrmacht, so she too was open to blackmail by the communists who saw an advantage in preying on their guilt and fear of reprisals.

When the two collaborators met for coffee, they always tried to snag a corner table near the window. Nevertheless, they had a fear of being overheard, so they'd invented code names for their most talked about targets. The Italian boarders as a group were known to them as the "di Medici Roses". The baker was the "Rise and Shine Rose", and the butcher was the "Coup de Gras". It was the butcher who actually kept an eye on the two Luxembourgers, as well as feeding them information and receiving it.

Yesterday, Frau Kolnberger had found a small note secreted in the neck cavity of the turkey she'd ordered. She almost missed it, but fortunately Herr Richter, the German butcher, had wrapped a twist of foil around it.

Since their conversation was supposedly concerning roses, an eavesdropper would have had a difficult time following their tortured dialogue. Today, while settled in just after one o'clock in the "Trois Cygnets" at their favorite dark wood, highly polished table, the two sat with their heads close together.

"The 'Coup de Gras' rose gave off such a sweet scent yesterday," began Gretta Kolnberger. "It was like a message from the magi of the east. In fact, it foretold a visit from such a magi."

Dieter understood that Gretta had a message through the butcher. The "magi of the east", however, eluded him. The communists were his best bet since they were east of here, but a visitor? What could that mean? This news threw his usually orderly thoughts into confusion. Would Gretta and he be asked to do more than eavesdrop? He liked passing along information because it was his nature to snoop. Knowing more than the average person on the street fed his need for a sense of superiority. In a rare moment of character assessment when his self-deception was allowed to slip, he knew he was just a little nondescript man who was too weak to stand up for any cause of freedom. He would serve whoever was the strongest master with the sharpest whip.

Today Gretta wished she had more to add to this exciting information. She wondered who was coming from the Eastern Bloc. Would it be a man or a woman? She hoped it would be a handsome, resolute comrade. She could conjure up his image. He'd be tall with disciplined posture—not like Herr Braun, sitting opposite her. Herr Braun looked slightly frightened by the butcher's news. She knew this evening he'd take refuge in his garden and discuss his fears with his roses. That would calm him; it always did.

That evening, after checking the windows, locking the vault and setting the alarm, Herr Braun bade good-bye to his co-workers as they left, locked the solid door of the bank and headed for home and his garden. Just the thought of his garden altered his blood pressure. Ever since his meeting with Frau Kolnberger, he'd felt nervous. His palms had been sweaty and had stuck to the currency bills as he counted them out in front of his customers. Every so often, he had turned to look over the grill of his cage, checking the clock that hung above the front door. Not fast enough. The time was passing too slowly. He wanted this day to be over.

Upon joining the flow of fellow pedestrians, he was swept along north towards the intersection with Rue du Bonnet. Turning left, he fell into step behind two young ladies in navy blue suits. Such young women dressed in conservative blue suits were not anything out of the ordinary here in the center of the business district. These two ladies, however, caught Dieter's attention because they wore shoulder-length blue veils and were conversing in English.

Dieter knew enough English and other languages to change the money that foreign travelers brought into his bank. Nevertheless, he could only make out a word here and there that the two women ahead of him were saying to each other. They laughed a lot he noticed, and the veils, he thought, must signify they were religious—modern religious. He didn't approve of the changes coming out of Rome these days. Especially he didn't like to see nuns about in the streets. They had convent walls to hide behind and ought to stay there.

Suddenly, the two nuns stopped in front of a store window that advertised "Metzgerei" in bold red letters. It was the butcher Herr Richter's shop, which stood out because of its German name. With Gilmary leading the way, the two entered the store. Naturally, now that Dieter was curious about them, he wandered into the shop too and stood inconspicuously next to a cabinet that held pickled goods. He expected the two nuns to try to do business in English and then start over again in French when they realized Herr Richter couldn't understand them.

Instead, Sister Gilmary began by greeting the butcher in German.

Herr Braun noticed how the butcher's expression became friendlier at hearing his native tongue. With care, the sturdy man in the blood-splattered apron took the slab of pork that Gilmary pointed out, trimmed it and cut it into chops. Unconsciously, as he wrapped the package of meat and secured it with string, Herr Richter began to hum *"Avanti o popolo"* under his breath. He liked young nuns, especially if they could speak German so well, as this one did.

Gilmary's ears perked up. She hadn't heard that melody since she'd left Italy. It was the melody to an Italian communist song. Why would a German butcher in Luxembourg City know that tune? Maybe he had fought in Italy during the war. Regardless, it was a catchy melody, and so she started to hum it with him.

Surprised at hearing her join in, Herr Richter scrutinized her closely and then observed her companion. He decided that the light-haired one looked more Teutonic with her blond hair sticking out of her veil and over her forehead. The one humming had auburn hair and dark, expressive eyebrows over green eyes— not a very Teutonic look. Maybe she was Italian. Whatever she was, she must be a comrade disguised as a nun. Could she be the agent that they were expecting from the communist headquarters? Is this the way an agent would announce her arrival—speaking German and humming a communist patriotic anthem? He wasn't sure of what to do next, so he just handed the package to her, took the money and made change.

The two nuns left the butcher's shop and joined the crowd on the sidewalk. Spying a bus at the corner, they boarded it quickly and continued home.

Herr Braun had never heard the Italian communist song, *"Avanti o popolo"*, so the significance of the nun humming it was lost on him. By the time Herr Richter had alerted him to follow the young nuns, he had lost their trail. He ran to the nearest corner and looked up, down, right and left. They were not there. Then he ran back past the shop to the other corner, again, no sign of them.

Reentering the butcher's shop, he waited until Herr Richter had time to talk to him. Finally the butcher had finished with his last customer of the day. Motioning to Dieter and in a conspiratorial tone, he said, "That young woman dressed as a nun must be the agent we are expecting from communist headquarters. She knew the sign and wanted to present herself to us so we would recognize her. I think she'll come here again now that she's certain we're her comrades."

A shiver of excitement ran through each man, but Dieter's excitement was heightened by fear.

Chapter Thirteen

Gilmary had ignored her rumbling stomach long enough. She was so hungry for lunch that she'd have to eat a real meal instead of her usual orange and hard-boiled egg. Just fifteen minutes previously, Maria Goretti had stuck her head into Gilmary's cubicle and announced she was going for lunch next door at the Chez Maurice Bistro. Gilmary said she'd join her as soon as she finished transcribing her shorthand into an offer to purchase in French for an Italian client. After she had it transcribed, she would hand it over to Monsieur Weicker, the solicitor, so he could check the legality of the document.

Walking the few steps to the bistro entrance, Gilmary pulled the door open and immediately the voices of a roomful of diners rising above the noise of the cutlery and crockery confronted her. Scanning the two rows of small tables, she failed to see her companion in her blue suit. In fact, every table had at least two people occupying it, so there were no empty seats.

Looking to her left, she saw a friendly young woman wearing a white apron motioning for her to follow her into the back room.

Adjusting her eyes to the comparable darkness of this room, she concluded that the majority of the people eating here were migrants who worked nearby in construction. She supposed at least a couple of them had come to see herself or Maria Goretti for translations in the last two weeks or so. For in the three weeks she and Maria Goretti had been working in their cubicles, business had quickly picked up as word of their expertise had traveled.

"Gilmary, over here!" she heard. Peering through the haze of cigarette smoke, Gilmary could make out the smiling face of Maria Goretti. She was motioning to an empty chair beside her at a table where the other seats were filled by four construction workers.

Moving closer to the table, she recognized Krzysztof, the Pole, who was their first customer. He and the others all held playing cards in their hands. Even Maria Goretti had a hand full of cards.

"What's going on here?" asked Gilmary, surprised at seeing her friend as the only woman seated in the back room with all of the migrants.

"We're having a game of sheepshead," replied Maria Goretti as she nodded to Krzysztof and the other three Poles. Rather apologetically she continued, "You see, they only had four players, and it's a much better game with five. I adore playing *'schafkopf'*, as it's called in German in Milwaukee. I played it at home with the family every Sunday while I was growing up. My Uncle Roland was the sharpest player I'd ever met until now. However, maybe I'll learn something new from playing with these fellows."

Gilmary just snorted her disbelief at what she was seeing. Right now, though, was not the time to show her disapproval of her friend's lunchtime companions and their game, so she just sat and watched them until they finished and were ready to order lunch.

Finally, one of the men called, "*schneider*," and the game was over. Then Maria Goretti made the introductions. As each man was introduced, he rose from his chair and made a little bow to Gilmary. They had great respect for the religious sisters.

Over sausages, sauerkraut, cheese, beer and swartzbrod, Gilmary mostly listened to the men and Maria Goretti converse together. After they laughed a lot about something Maria Goretti had said, Gilmary asked Krzysztof in German for an explanation. Krzysztof hesitated, but finally answered in German. He sheepishly explained that some Poles knew German, but were reluctant to speak it because they harbored such distaste for the Nazis, who had occupied their country during World War II.

Gilmary nodded in understanding. Poor Poland had gone from bad to worse, for when they finally got rid of the Germans, they turned around to find themselves on a leash, tethered to the Russians. A bad deal no matter how one looked at it.

"We're the lucky ones," explained Krzysztof as he pointed to himself and waved his right hand towards his companions. "Although we work hard at jobs that are often dangerous, we can do whatever we like when we don't work— like play cards with Siostra Maria Goretti and drink beer." Then he winked at Gilmary and laughed heartily.

Gilmary laughed too, but less heartily since she didn't think playing cards with Polish workers would pass muster with Mother Assumpta. What was Maria Goretti thinking, she wondered?

Later that evening, Gilmary asked Maria Goretti why she was playing cards in the back room. "At least you weren't smoking a stogie with the men," she snickered.

Rather defensively, Maria Goretti explained that she enjoyed it, but more importantly, she was viewing it as an apostolate to the workers. She felt that if they accepted her as a friend, she could urge them to practice their faith in this foreign land.

"In Poland, it's difficult to openly observe their faith, so I'll tell them that here they can show how proud they can be of being both Christian and Polish. They like the freedom here. Maybe we can have Mass in Polish at some church that caters to migrants, and after Mass we can all play sheepshead!" This thought caused a blissful smile to spread over Maria Goretti's face.

Gilmary could only sigh and squeeze her friend's hand. To each their own, she thought. She had espionage, and Maria Goretti had a Polish apostolate. Who knew which circle of Dante's paradise they would eventually occupy? She fervently hoped there'd be room there for some spies and lots of Poles.

Chapter Fourteen

Olga Diederich stood at the railing looking down into the deep valley below. Because it was just past noon, there were few shadows, so she was able to see the Petrusse River rolling along merrily. Behind her the last of the parishioners was leaving the cathedral after attending the final Sunday Mass. She herself had attended all three of the Masses beginning at 7:30 in the morning—not, of course, out of piety, but because she was looking for a young nun in a white habit. She hadn't found her in any of the crowds of worshipers, and that had her discouraged. What she had seen was a total cross-section of the inhabitants of Luxembourg City. There in the soaring space of the cathedral, burgermeisters and migrants had stood and knelt shoulder to shoulder. Olga marveled at how egalitarian everyone was in church. She doubted if such behavior carried over into their lives the rest of the week. Like most of the western societies, there seemed to be a hierarchy of classes, from the families with old titles to the newly arrived immigrants—surely a stuffy class system, of which she strongly disapproved. She preferred the planned society in the Eastern Bloc countries, at least in theory.

Just then a trim, middle-aged woman in a chic, green suit caught her attention. She was leading a group of tourists into the entrance to the underground labyrinth of caverns called the Casemates. Curious about these ancient fortifications, Olga skipped quickly down the steps to join the queue of tourists.

Plunking down her money, she got her ticket and joined

73

the group just as the guide was introducing herself in German. Good, Olga thought, I've joined the German-speaking group.

"*Guten tag*," began the lady. "*Ich bin Tilly*." After her introduction, she continued by explaining the expansiveness of the series of underground rooms they were about to explore.

"Twenty-three kilometers or fourteen miles is the length of these connected tunnels. But don't worry, I won't make you walk and climb through all of those kilometers. Since the late 1800s, many miles of the labyrinth have been filled in or blocked from entry, so that no army in the future will be tempted to occupy them again."

Behind her, Olga heard an old man with a cane say, "Thank goodness for that!"

"You see," continued Tilly, "whichever army held these Casemates, which can hold many thousands of soldiers, horses and weapons, could control the whole northwest of Europe. That's why this strategic position was known as the 'Gibraltar of the North' ever since the Spanish invaders in 1644 enlarged the modest cellars under the original castle into these miles of caverns."

For the better part of an hour, the group of German tourists followed Tilly and marveled at the large series of hollowed-out rooms that had apertures for cannons overlooking the Petrusse River. It was hard to conceive how these rooms went on for mile upon mile.

When they came to the end of the tour and the group turned around to follow Tilly as they retraced their steps back to the entrance, Olga hung back and inspected the rough walls, trying to see where the rest of the series of caverns had been sealed. In the shadows she discerned an area of smooth surface with four large indented circles, each holding a strong metal ring. Rubbing her hands over the dark smoothness, she came to two pairs of large hinges. Now she understood. There were two large doors in the wall which, when opened by the metal rings, would allow large machines to enter and exit.

Then she smiled as a clever thought crossed her mind. What if those sealed caverns held a large cache of weapons? She'd heard the western European countries supposedly had organized and armed "stay-behind" armies. These so-called armies were a clandestine creation of NATO and the American CIA. Undoubtedly, these hidden caverns would be a perfect place to store weapons. Just now at the end of the tour, the guide had pointed out that the locked iron gate before them separated the long line of tunnels they had passed through from a wide ramp which veered off at a right angle and eventually led to the street above. Excitedly, Olga thought that such an exit ramp meant men could access and dispense the weapons quickly from their underground hiding place.

Now she wondered if the local Soviet agents had considered that this might be the site of a hidden cache. Certainly, she reasoned, NATO could store an enormous amount of weapons here—more than the Luxembourg secret army could use. Ah, she thought, there would have to be weapons here so that if Americans and British forces came to help protect this area from Soviet expansion, many of their armaments would already be in place.

Excited that she might have come up with some possibly valuable information for her Soviet handlers, Olga left the gloom of the caverns and resurfaced onto the sunlit Rue de la Constitution. The brightness hurt her eyes until they adjusted, and she continued along the street towards the business center of town.

Now close to two o'clock, the wind had picked up. It blew small swirls of dust up from the gutters onto the sidewalk. Ahead of her, she observed a gaggle of the German tourists from her group that had just toured the Casemates. They had stopped in front of a butcher's shop and were talking to the beefy proprietor, who was trying to close up his shop. He had only been open for a couple of hours so the city folks could pick up the meat they had ordered for their Sunday dinners. But now the German tourists had waylaid him and were asking about restaurants.

Olga joined the group. When the German butcher saw her, he stopped in mid-sentence and stared. Here was the young nun he had seen in his shop the other day. Only today she was not dressed as a modern nun. Did she have more information or orders for him?

As the group of tourists moved on, Herr Richter motioned to Olga to enter his shop as he turned the sign in the door so it read "Closed" in Luxembourg, German and French. Then Comrade Richter began to hum *"Avanti o popolo"* lightly under his breath.

Olga picked up on it and adjusted the red scarf she was wearing on her head.

"E come una bandiera rossa, signorina," he said with a wink, liking her scarf to the red Communist flag.

Looking at him in amazement, the Stasi assassin wondered how he knew Italian. Of course, she thought, he would have to know enough to sell meat to the many Italian workmen and their families, who had immigrated here from the south of Italy.

Now with a wide smile and waving a plump finger at her, the butcher pointed to her scarf and teased her. "You've changed your blue veil today for a red flag. Good choice!" For he was sure that it was the same young woman who had come in with a companion near closing time the other day. Both women had been dressed as nuns. Today however, this one had a red-patterned skirt, white blouse and under her red scarf, her hair was blonde. She had auburn hair the other day. But one of them had been blonde, and since he had only seen them for a short time, perhaps he had mixed them up.

Olga was trying to put the puzzle together. "Oh, was I

wearing a black veil the last time we met? Was my dress white? I have several disguises, you know."

Herr Richter began to think that this woman was too forgetful to be a top-notch spy. "Don't you recall? You and your friend were dressed in blue suits like modern nuns. Your blue suit is okay, but I think an old-fashioned habit is a better disguise."

Olga had found a new piece of the puzzle. So that explained why she had not found the Dominican, who looked to be her double. The real religious had exchanged her long, white dress for a blue suit. But where was she now?

"I see you're an observant man. Our cause needs more men like you. I have important information and have to pass it along to the right party. Do you have a commandant here in Luxembourg who relays your information to East Berlin or Moscow?"

Herr Richter began to wonder how this comrade had washed up on his shore. She seemed to operate outside of the usual network. But maybe she was testing him. He would send her along to Dieter Braun and see what he thought of her. Regardless, he decided, she was not the top level comrade who had been promised to them.

"Fraulein, you must go to the Freistadt Bank in the morning and ask to see Herr Dieter Braun. He may be able to direct you."

Chapter Fifteen

On Monday morning, Dieter Braun said good-bye to his roses and began the walk to the bank. Since it was a very fine spring morning, he decided to take a route past the formal garden next to the cathedral.

Yes, he'd been right to go out of his way to see the garden. Its roses were just beginning to open. He most admired the yellow ones with the subtle rose blush. He knew that after they had basked a while in the warmth of the sun, they'd reward onlookers with an aroma as heady as fine wine.

Turning the corner and entering the street where his bank was located, he suddenly realized he was following two young women in blue suits again. They also had short, blue veils. Excitedly, he tried to walk faster so he could come abreast of them and see their faces. Just as he came up even with them, they turned and entered the lobby for the law offices of Weicker and Franck. He stopped and watched through the window as the women each entered a glassed-in cubicle set in the lobby. Above one cubicle, a sign proclaimed "Polish translation". The other advertised "Italian, French and German translation". Now he knew. These two women were scribes, who could write letters for migrants or translate documents for them, and one of them was an undercover communist agent.

Later that morning, Dieter was in his cage at the bank when a young blonde woman wearing a red scarf approached him. When he looked into her eyes, he recognized her and marveled at how quickly she could change her disguise. Three hours ago, he had seen her in her blue nun's garb. Now here she was before him in a skirt, blouse, and scarf.

"Are you Herr Dieter Braun?" Olga asked in German.

"Yes, I am," he answered deferentially, for he felt that she might be the agent from East Berlin that they were anticipating.

Olga slid a stack of Italian lire under the grill towards him. "Could you convert this into Luxembourg francs?"

As Dieter worked on the transaction, Olga very quietly told him of her meeting with Herr Richter. Then she asked the banker for a communist contact. Looking up surprised, he decided she must not be the East Berliner they were expecting.

"We are waiting for someone to arrive very soon from Berlin. When that agent reveals himself to us, I'll let you know immediately. I saw you going to work this morning, so I know where to find you. You are being quite clever to be dressed as a nun and acting as a scribe." Dieter smiled ingratiatingly. "I congratulate you on your language skills."

Ah, just as she thought. Her doppelganger was a linguist and a scribe. Now she just had to find out where she worked.

After thanking him and tucking her Luxembourg money into her volcano bag, she strolled out onto the street. Looking to her right, she spotted a tourist information sign four doors further up the street.

Five minutes later, Olga exited the tourist office, pocketing a guidebook and map of the countryside. Crossing the street, she turned onto Rue du Bonnet and saw what she had hoped to find, a sign for Weicker and Franck, attorneys and scribes.

Now she felt she was nearing the end of her search. The next problem was how to corner and kill her doppelganger. Only when she was eliminated could Olga regain her reputation and rightful place in the communist spy network.

Chapter Sixteen

Salzburg, Austria

Genevieve von Hollenden looked past the Pegasus fountain, with its cascading waters sparkling in the sunlight, towards the Hohensalzburg Castle across the Salzach River. She sighed with pleasure and in annoyance. Salzburg was always delightful, and had been the city that she and her husband enjoyed the most when they toured several European cities the summer of 1950. Back then she was more captivated by the city's music and connection to Mozart, than its renowned roses.

Now, fifteen years later, it was the roses and caches of weapons that had brought her here. Salzburg had at least two noteworthy rose gardens so she should be able to truly immerse herself in the study of each of them, that is, if it weren't for the pesky man at her side.

He just did not inspire confidence—not from the time she had met him at the hotel, nor now in the garden. Certainly, he looked the part of a rose garden enthusiast, with his yellow blush boutonniere threaded jauntily through the buttonhole of his lapel.

That morning, previous to his appearance at her hotel, a bouquet of gorgeous roses had been delivered to her room. The accompanying card proclaimed, "Compliments to Madame von Hollenden. Welcome to Salzburg, a city of roses." It was signed in a flourishing script by Jurgen Adler and the Salzburg Roseniers.

Later in the lobby, a tall, lightly-tanned gentleman in his

forties had risen from his chair when she exited the elevator. With his hat in hand, he had bowed slightly and introduced himself as Jurgen Adler. Looking up into his face, she saw alert, dark eyes under slightly drooping eyelids. His smile, visibly polite, lacked genuine warmth. Nevertheless, like a well-mannered gentleman, he had offered her his arm and led her out to his car.

First, he took her to the Rosenhugel Gardens, overlooking the Mirabell Park. Since it was early May, the rose bushes were just beginning to set blooms. One could glimpse the color of the unfolding flowers as their buds swelled with the promise of a glorious display.

Genevieve had carefully looked over some of the plants, examining them closely for any sign of the botrytis blight. The trigger sentences for discussing where to hide the "stay-behind" army's cache of weapons were supposed to concern diseases of rose plants. Botrytis blight was a common problem for rose bushes. She only hoped she could find some here, but wasn't confident that she would in such a well-tended garden.

In a corner of the garden near a stone wall, where a row of tea roses were positioned in the shade during the morning, she finally found faint evidence of the disease.

Bending down to examine the plant, Genevieve said, "I see this plant has signs of the botrytis blight. It must be caused by the dew not evaporating early enough in the day, keeping the plant damp and encouraging mold." Then she looked up at Jurgen Adler and waited for his response. She expected he'd continue with more information on diseases affecting the tea rose.

Instead of affirming her observation and expanding on it, he looked slightly confused and bored. Coughing into his cuffed fist, he looked over at the veranda to their left and observed, "We would do better to walk over there where the plants are already in full sunlight." And so they had strolled to the veranda in silence.

A half hour later, now in the main part of the Mirabell

Gardens, Genevieve tried again. "What do the members of your rose society recommend to eradicate the Japanese beetle? In Luxembourg we control them by taking a dish of soapy water and tapping the bush until they fall into the dish. It seems to work best either early in the morning or later in the day towards dusk."

This time Jurgen stared down at her and observed, "We don't have any Japanese beetles here. Our roses are all perfectly healthy. The freshness of our mountain air and the healthy level of humidity are what contribute to the general good health of our people and our plants."

Genevieve thought that he wasn't playing along. She felt like an actress whose fellow actor had forgotten his lines and was ad-libbing. The problem was that his ad-libbing changed the plot. He and she seemed to be in two different plays. It certainly wasn't what she had expected. Why, she asked herself—why isn't he volunteering information? Could it be that he knows nothing about roses? Then he is surely not the man with whom I'm supposed to discuss weapon caches.

Trying to appear relaxed and natural, she was nevertheless on guard. Luckily, she hadn't mentioned that she'd been to Salzburg previously with her husband. It was better to appear that this was a first-time experience.

Turning to the Austrian and giving him a warm smile, Genevieve covered up her distrust by saying, "These gardens are oriented towards that castle on the small mountain across the river, aren't they?"

Jurgen turned towards the enormous fortress that brooded over the city below it. "The Prince Archbishop Wolf Dietrich reigned over there in the Hohensalzburg Castle at the beginning of the 17th century, but his mistress reigned down here in this bowery. That palace over there next to this garden was built for her. In that way, whenever she walked in the garden, her gaze was directed upwards towards the imposing home of her benefactor."

Turning back to look at Genevieve, Jurgen quickly said, "That reminds me of the next garden that you must see this afternoon. Beyond the castle mountain, there's another garden that the Prince Archbishop Marcus Sitticus had laid out for his pleasure and that of his guests—for he entertained continuously. The park is called Hellbrun and it's a place no tourist should miss. Besides its roses, there are surprises in its man-made grottos. I know you'll like it, so we'll go there after lunch."

The Austrian's eyes showed more life now, and he spoke with enthusiasm. So far, he had not found the switch that would get this Luxembourg lady to discuss weapons. Maybe he should try charm, although charm wasn't his strong suite—physical force was what he preferred. It achieved quicker results.

For lunch, he had chosen to take her to St. Peter Keller, a unique restaurant located in a cavern at the foot of the Festungsberg Mountain upon which the castle stood. He thought the intriguing atmosphere of the cavern might open the conversation to hidden caches. His job was to place himself as the credible agent to receive the NATO weapons. If he was successful in gaining this lady's confidence, he could have the weapons delivered right into the waiting hands of the Soviet agents operating in this part of Austria. Then the local "stay-behind" army would be severely limited as far as weapons if it ever came to an armed conflict between the Soviets and the local freedom fighters.

Genevieve looked around with real pleasure at the waiters bustling about the subtly-lighted cavern room. It certainly was enjoyable to be back here in old Salzburg. She had eaten here before, fifteen years ago, and the familiar decor and atmosphere delighted her. It was sometimes comforting to find your favorite things unchanged. In fact, the menu seemed to be the same as she remembered it also.

Jurgen watched her carefully as a smile played around his lips. Thoughtfully, he ran his forefinger over his small, dark moustache. She looked relaxed and defenseless as she examined the menu. Now he could steer the conversation towards hidden caches.

"Don't you find this cavern evocative, Genevieve? May I call you Genevieve? Madame von Hollenden seems so formal, and we do both share the same passion for roses."

Genevieve smiled sweetly, but thought that, while she had a certain passion for the flowers, he had not done a believable job of demonstrating his passion for them.

"Yes, Jurgen, do call me Genevieve. Are there many of these caverns on the side of this mountain?"

Finally Jurgen felt they were on the right subject. "Many. A few have been used for centuries to store and keep cool the barrels of beer from the breweries—or cure slabs of meat. Others were used as burial sites. Probably the first humans who roamed this area lived in caverns. I wonder what the people of our century will use them for." (He, of course, pictured them filled with caches of guns and ammunition).

Genevieve nodded diffidently. "I suppose they'll go on cooling beer and curing meat in them, don't you?" Then she turned her attention to the waiter, who stood patiently attentive a short distance from their table.

Later, during dessert, Jurgen tried another, more direct tack. "I'm sure you know the Soviets control the eastern part of Austria and have a strong desire to take over the rest of the country. Our people here don't want to see that happen. If only we had weapons for the patriots, then we would feel secure, knowing we could protect ourselves." While saying this, the Austrian tried to look slightly beseeching and perplexed at the same time.

Madame von Hollenden stirred sugar and cream into her coffee and looked at him sympathetically, shaking her head. "I find this business of politics too complex. Grayer heads than mine can puzzle it out. Just so we don't muddle into another war.

That would be unthinkable!"

There, she thought, I've blocked his advance by playing dumb. What can he say to that!

By the time Genevieve and Jurgen reached Hellbrun, the Austrian was almost convinced that the Luxembourg lady was not a connection to NATO, but only an attractive, middle-aged and rather vacuous matron. Someone had been misinformed about her and believed it. She really only knew about roses. Her interest had been aroused when she had discovered a Luxembourger rose in the Mirabell Gardens, for that was what she had come to find. She had supposed he would know more about the provenance of many of the plants and seemed disappointed at his lack of knowledge.

Right now he felt like an unwilling chaperon, one who had to pretend his way through yet another rose garden. Why, he wondered, were Salzburgers so enthusiastic about these damn flowers? At least there were the trick water fountains to surprise her.

Entering the first grotto with a surprise fountain, Genevieve, who had seen them all before on her previous visit with her husband, expressed astonishment and delight. "Oh, Jurgen, how ingenious that old archbishop and his engineers were back then. What tricks he could play on his guests. I wonder how many ever came back to his later parties. They must have brought umbrellas with them after their first visit! Or maybe they declined the invitation on account of contracting pneumonia."

Jurgen didn't even smile at such levity—his feet were starting to tire. Also, he was feeling tightness behind his eyes. He knew it was the beginning of a headache.

As they came into the next grotto, he looked longingly at the stone stools grouped around a long table made of the same stone. There were ten smaller stools, with a more prominent one at the head of the table. From this stool, the Prince Archbishop had surveyed his seated guests and relished their consternation at his planned surprise.

Right now, however, that seat was occupied by a small boy, who would need years to grow into his role at the head of the table. A girl, slightly older than the boy, was standing on another of the stools and starting to jump to the next one. As she jumped from stool to stool, she recited a rhyme in a sing-song voice.

Jurgen sank onto an empty stool, not caring that he was impeding the girl's journey around the table.

"Herr, Herr, bitte!" she said in an irritated voice, but Jurgen just waved a tired and dismissive back of his hand in her general direction.

Genevieve recognized this grotto and remembered its hidden possibilities. It was here that the 17th century archbishop indulged in his amusement to the chagrin of his guests. She knew Jurgen would be familiar with the trick fountains, but he didn't know that she had experienced them before today.

"Jurgen, you look exhausted, and you deserve a rest after all of the walking we've done. You've done a splendid job of showing me the sights that I wanted to see, but now I need to find a rest room. There has to be one nearby, so just stay put here until I return in a couple of minutes."

Genevieve turned back on the path towards the direction from which they had entered the grotto and disappeared behind some boulders. Sneaking back to an alcove in the grotto, she spied the faucet she was hoping to find. It was housed in a small, gray box, whose door did not squeak when she opened it. Quickly she turned the metal knob and heard the swish of squirting water. That sound was followed by squeals of delightful surprise. Genevieve could imagine the young girl getting wet while her brother sat in satisfied dryness in the archbishop's chair. After all, the archbishop could not get drenched, only his unsuspecting guests.

But what about Jurgen? He was her real target. Then she knew his fate as she heard heavy oaths sworn in Russian and

German being hurled towards the heavens. Satisfied that she had uncovered his true nature, she quickly shut off the water and silently slipped out of the alcove and hurried away to a small building nearby. It was not the rest room, but at least she could hide there for a couple of minutes before backtracking to the wet grotto to view her handiwork.

Two minutes later, she feigned shock and surprise when she rounded the boulders and came upon a disgruntled, wet Jurgen. At that moment, he sat on the damp table, while the pools of water around the soaked stools drained into their subterranean channels.

"Jurgen! What happened?"

Jurgen only gritted his teeth and tried to control his rage. Then he stood up and bowed, saying, "As you can see, the archbishop, although having been dead for four hundred years, can still play his little tricks."

Genevieve looked at his wet hat, jacket, pants legs and shoes. He did look an unhappy mess.

He continued, "It's a cool day—too cool to stay in wet clothing, so I think our tour of the gardens has ended. I'll return you to your hotel, Madame." With a violent nod of his head, he snapped his heels together, which sprayed some water from his shoes.

Oh, he's really mad, thought the Luxembourger. He's trying to control his anger by resorting to formality. She actually felt a twinge of conscience. Was it necessary to make him mad? Yes, she decided. He was trying to deceive her into confiding top-secret information. He deserved a dousing.

The ride back from the Hellbrun gardens had been silent on Jurgen's part. Genevieve tried to express her concern and had urged him to have a warm drink as soon as possible. At the hotel entrance, she jumped quickly out of the car in order to save him the embarrassment of getting out and opening the door for her. It would have done his ego no good to be seen wet and disheveled.

At the last moment, she extended her hand and thanked him for the lovely day. He waved off both her hand and her remark, and drove off briskly, squealing his tires in the process.

As soon as she entered her room, she looked for a telephone book, found the number for a large garden shop, and phoned it. A pert, young voice answered in German, *"Guten tag"*.

Genevieve responded, "Hello, I'm a visitor to Salzburg and an admirer of your outstanding rose gardens. Could you tell me who the president is of your local rose society? I would love to get advice from that person."

The woman's voice on the other end of the line hesitated. Finally, with a touch of sadness, she responded. "I'm sorry, Madame, Jurgen Adler was the president of our rose society. Unfortunately, you've come too late to Salzburg to speak with him. He died three days ago; he was hit by a car while crossing the Langenstrasse. No one saw the car coming until it was upon him. In fact, the car had just pulled away from the curb as he stepped into the street. It was so tragic and unexpected!"

Genevieve was stunned. After thanking the woman for the information, she stood looking at the telephone receiver still grasped in her hand. Slowly she returned it to its cradle. Who was the man who had been passing himself off as Jurgen? The thought of how she had spent the whole day with him sent shivers down her back. Reflecting on how she'd felt he was all wrong for being her "stay-behind" army's contact, she sighed with relief that she hadn't voiced her doubt. She hoped he'd concluded that he'd wasted a day with an innocent, Luxembourgish rose-enthusiast.

But how had anyone except herself, some NATO or CIA agent and the real Jurgen Adler known about her true reason for visiting Salzburg? Loose lips could do more than sink ships; they could derail plans for getting weapon cache shipments into the right hands.

Grabbing her suitcase and throwing it onto the bed, she began to toss her clothes, toiletries and shoes into it. In less than five minutes, she was at the reception desk paying her bill and ordering a taxi. At the door, she tipped the doorman, who put her suitcase in the trunk of the taxi and deposited her into the cab, and then she sped away to the train station. If she was lucky, she could still be in Munich by dinnertime and then on the night train north towards Luxembourg City. The thought of home never seemed sweeter!

Chapter Seventeen

Luxembourg City

The last few days had found Gilmary translating for two Italian laborers—brothers Giuseppe and Rocco Balistrero. The first day they came for help, they were light-hearted and joking with her, but the second day they entered her cubicle nervously with their caps in their hands. After explaining to them her translation of their documents, she put down the papers and eyed them with concern.

"You both look worried. Are things not going well for you here? Yesterday you both seemed so light-hearted. What changed?"

Rocco looked at his brother and sighed heavily. He doubted a young nun would understand the intricacies of politics, but since she looked so concerned, he'd try to explain.

"Where we come from, *Sorella*, the communists are very active. People in our part of Calabria respect them because they have social programs that help some of the poor. Here you don't see the communists. If they existed here, we didn't know it until last night."

"What happened last night?" Gilmary was very much alert now. She suspected the German butcher was a communist and might be a conduit for her to find an agent who would accept her in her role as Olga Diederich, the Stasi assassin. But there had to be a network of socialists at work here, not just one man.

"Last night a man from behind the Iron Curtain—he said

Berlin—came to our social club. We meet weekly and sometimes more often just to exchange news from home and share our favorite Italian foods. Giuseppe and I look forward to it and always have fun. But this man, who wasn't Italian, was trying to sign us up as communists here in our guest country. He said we owed it to our countrymen to further communism here too. But I think it is trouble for us to be communist here.

"The Luxembourg people treat us good now, but if we try to organize as communists, they may throw us out. It's a bad business and he scared us. Giuseppe and I left before we would feel forced to sign up. It spoiled our evening, and many of us felt shaken by it."

Gilmary looked at each man and gauged their fear. "I think you were right to leave the meeting and not get mixed up in communist politics. Luxembourgers would definitely send you home if you publically agitated for communism. We're a free and democratic people." Then she stood and shook hands with them.

Just then her stomach rumbled loud enough that the men smiled. Gilmary laughed and excused her impolite noises.

"Come and join us for lunch next door," they offered.

Looking over towards Maria Goretti's cubicle, she saw that her friend had already left. No doubt she was playing cards in the smoke-filled back room. Of course, she was also saving souls—just not in a prescribed manner.

"I'd like that," she accepted.

As the three of them entered the dim room that was buzzing with men's voices talking animatedly in Polish, Italian and Portuguese, Rocco suddenly stopped. Gilmary sensed his reluctance to continue and followed the direction of his gaze. The young Italian was frowning at a middle-aged man in a black suit, who was seated at a long table next to the wall. The other men seated there were Italian laborers in overalls. Waving and calling amiably to Rocco and his brother, the Italians wanted

91

them to join their group.

"That's the man from last night," Giuseppe said tensely.

Gilmary paused to try to decide if it would be wise to meet this communist agent now, or should she prepare herself first for her initial encounter with him. She had hesitated too long though. Now the man in the black suit had seen the three of them, and rising from his chair, he motioned them to join their table. Three of the Italian men moved to the other end of the table so that Gilmary, Giuseppe and Rocco could sit next to the agent.

It must be preordained, thought the nun. She tried to smile as they took their seats next to the Berliner, but it was probably more of a grimace. She was nervous and had to gauge whether she should tip her hand to this agent or stay put in her role as a nun working as a scribe. Of course, the Italians would be scandalized if they thought she was a socialist, especially after her pretty speech about the free and democratic Luxembourgers. Wisely, she decided to play the religious role for now.

Speaking in Italian, the Berliner asked the nun about her work. While she replied, Gilmary studied him. He was of average height, but quite muscular. Intelligent too, she perceived. Probably the force of his personality made him a good leader of men. No wonder he had been sent to organize the workers here. Too bad for the Italians who listened to him. Their time working in Luxembourg could be cut short. Certainly their relatives back home, dependent on their transferred money, would not be happy to see them return.

After all the Italians had eaten, they rose to return to their jobs. Gilmary, however, lingered, talking to Herr Feldmeier, as she had come to know the agent from Berlin.

Finally they were alone at the table. Looking over to where Maria Goretti had been eating with the Polish workers, she saw that they had left too.

Turning back to Herr Feldmeier, she addressed him in

German. "My name is really Olga Diederich, and I was trained by the Stasi, although I now work for the Soviets. Our organization here has need of a leader like you. There's information I have that has to be channeled back to Berlin and on to Moscow. It concerns the cache of weapons for the 'stay-behind' army here in Luxembourg."

The Berliner felt surprised that he would be approached so directly by a nun. Her demeanor and disguise were excellent deception. He really had accepted her as a religious upon being introduced to her. Who would suspect her of being a Stasi agent? What a gift to the Party to have her planted here, in the middle of all of these migrants, and accepted as a pious religious. He knew these migrants had great respect for nuns and priests. They would listen to her, even if they would not listen to him. If the Communist Party could co-opt all of the priests and nuns in southern Europe, their take-over would be the easiest revolution in all of history. In reality, however, the Catholic Church had taken a determined stand against communism and its atheistic principle. Nevertheless, this pretend nun seated before him, was a lost soul to the Church but a boon to the socialist cause.

Smiling encouraging at her, Feldmeier pulled his chair closer. "I'm pleased to meet such an accomplished agent. To have embedded yourself here as a religious in a position of trust is an espionage coup. Also, you must be congratulated on having already gleaned such important information. This is too public of a place, however, for us to discuss more—especially the particulars of the weapons. You know the city well, I suspect, so where can we meet privately?"

Gilmary thought past his immediate question to how she could use him to ferret out other agents here in the city. "I'll need to prepare for such a meeting since, of course, I don't live alone. Give me a contact person, and I'll get word to you through him when I'm ready for our meeting."

The Berliner hated to name another agent in the

espionage chain, but at the same time, he needed to know where the "stay-behinds" had secreted their stash. If he could forward such information on to Moscow, his standing in the Party would be enhanced. He wouldn't even have to mention that he found it out from this agent. After thinking about it, he decided he would give her the name of the agent he deemed weakest—Herr Braun. It would be better if she didn't know about the butcher because he was more valuable to the cause.

"If you go to the Freistadt Bank, there is a teller named Dieter Braun. He will be our conduit for messages. Tell him when and where we should meet, and he'll get the message to me. It's better if we aren't seen together anymore in public, since the migrants know that I'm here to organize them into communist cells."

Gilmary thought it was wise to not meet him again at all, but knew it was necessary and that the meeting must be planned carefully. It was time for a conference with Peter. He'd been gone to Rome again for two weeks. In fact, he had left quickly just after her mother returned from Salzburg. She wondered about the timing. Uncharacteristically, her mother seemed nervous upon her return and had spent time with Peter behind closed doors. Of course, it could just be that she was nervous about Nathan and sending him to America. Certainly it was understandable.

Chapter Eighteen

Salzburg, Austria

Stepping gracefully out of her front door and onto the stoop in front of her small house, Renata Friedhof saw Klaus out of the corner of her eye as she bent to put the old-fashioned key in the lock and turn it. "Drats", she uttered under her breath as she heard the click of the cylinder. He simply made her skin crawl every time she saw him. If it weren't for the money he intermittently paid her, she would pretend he wasn't there.

Nonchalantly smoking a cigarette, Klaus watched the well-endowed Renata leave her house and begin her evening promenade. He wasn't her sole admirer; several middle-aged and older men gathered most evenings just after the Angelus bells rang and waited eagerly for her appearance. For the uninitiated men, who just happened to be walking with their wives past this corner, it was an unexpected delight to see Renata sashay down the street towards the city center. Of course, the wives might enjoy seeing her drindl dress—the local costume that was quite becoming, but each grabbed her husband's arm more tightly when they noticed their man's wandering eyes enjoying more than the costume.

While leisurely strolling down the street, Renata was conscious of the pleasure she derived from all of the male attention. Even the envious women gave her satisfaction. She couldn't count many women as friends, but she understood and accepted that such was the price of her attentions.

Stopping at a bench in front of the Residenzplatz fountain, she seductively lifted her left leg and straightened the seam in her stocking. She wore the old-fashioned hosiery because it seemed to be more authentic with her Austrian dress. Also, straightening it was a sign for Klaus, who had followed her. It let him know she would meet him in their usual assignation— the mausoleum in the St. Sebastian's Cemetery. First, however, she moved into the shadow of the cathedral, where the flower vendors were packing up the bouquets they hadn't sold today.

"Good evening, Renata. Are you coming for a bouquet to take to the cemetery? I still have wonderful tulips in several colors. They're reduced now, so why not take two? You are good to remember your grossmutter with flowers."

"Yes, Lena, I'll take two of your bouquets. Did you know my grossmutter? I loved her very much since she was both mother and father to me. Taking flowers to her grave is all I can do for her now."

"Of course, I remember her. She often came here to buy flowers for your parents' graves. You are just like her." Then Lena stopped. Actually, she thought, Renata was not at all like her plain and sweet oma. While her grossmutter had lived a simple life and sought no attention, her granddaughter was just the opposite. It just shows, she thought, that families can have strange off-spring.

Fifteen minutes later, Renata entered the ancient cemetery, a large green space surrounded on all sides by family tombs, sheltered on the perimeter by an over-hanging roof. The whole of the quiet enclave was further surrounded by the church, a hostel, and some hotels and apartments that overlooked the entire cemetery. Walking to her family's gravesite, she paused at the stone that had attached to it an oval photo of an old lady behind glass. "I'm here, Oma. I'm a survivor. That's all that you asked of me—to be a survivor. How I survive is another matter, but you didn't specify how to do it. It's enough that I live."

Then she laid down the tulips and blew a kiss towards the photo. The two graves next to her grandmother's didn't merit any attention. They were her parents' graves, but she'd never known them. Slowly, she began to stroll into the shadow of the covered tombs. The whistle had blown that signaled the cemetery was closing for the day. Dodging behind a large tomb, she crouched and waited for the watchman to disappear. From behind the next tomb, she heard slightly labored breathing—Klaus. He would also be hidden until all was quiet.

A few minutes later, dusk had fallen completely over the quiet quadrangle. The two shadows, Klaus and Renata, silently crept to the circular mausoleum in the center of the cemetery. Klaus had a key for the large tomb's door, and it turned effortlessly, allowing the door to swing open. The interior was saved from total darkness by the votive candles flickering in the gloom, so Renata found a seat to the left of the door and eased onto it. Immediately, Klaus came and sat beside her. Not liking to have him so close, Renata slid further down the bench while wishing that she did not have to be here. Nevertheless, it was business and she needed it to survive.

"I see you had your usual trail of admirers tonight. You haven't lost your touch with the older crowd," observed an amused Klaus with a smile that he thought was rakish.

Renata winced at the words "older crowd". She accepted the fact she skirted close to middle-age, but certainly the allure of her beauty attracted attention from males of all ages. It was her greatest asset and would see her through to old age. She couldn't imagine life without all of the attention she'd gotten so accustomed to.

"Klaus! Don't try to critique me. I know myself and my art, so let's leave it at that! What's the business tonight? Do you have something for me to deliver? Maybe I can still get it done this evening."

The awkward man sighed. He could never seem to score with women. He still smarted with humiliation at the lack of success with the rose society lady from Luxembourg. At that time, he had assumed the role of Jurgen Adler, the late president of the local rose society. Luckily he had not contracted a severe cold from that escapade in the Hellbrun gardens. Worse yet, he still didn't know who the CIA had as their contact here in Salzburg. They had to have someone who could oversee the deployment of the weapons for the "stay-behind" army. Who was that person? And where were they going to hide the weapons? These questions burned at the forefront of his thoughts.

Focusing on the flickering red lights of the votive candles, Klaus considered that Renata was right to get down to business. The problem before them was urgent. "First, I have a message for you to deliver to Franz at the Liebestraum Hotel. As you know, he works during the day so you can wait until tomorrow to hand it over to him. Next, you'll have to use some of your fabled charm to approach an American who is coming from Rome and will be staying at the Liebestraum. Our contact in Rome thinks he's CIA, but isn't sure. For some time we've been expecting someone connected with them to come to Salzburg and oversee the current shipment of weapons for the secret 'stay-behind' army that NATO and the CIA have been forming since 1947. The man's name is Peter MacAllister. He's young, maybe a little out of your league, but if you approach him in the evening in dimmer light he may think that you're younger. I hear that the strong light of day is the enemy of beautiful women."

Renata stiffened at his rudeness. How clumsy he was! Oh how she wished she didn't have to tolerate his company— ever! Nevertheless, she accepted the two envelopes he handed to her. One was the packet he wanted delivered to Franz; the other her payment.

They left in silence and parted on Linzer Gasse after Klaus had let them out through the old, ornate gate of the cemetery, to which he had a key. He had keys to many places in Salzburg. It was amazing what money spread around in the right places could do for you.

The next morning, Renata left her modest house at ten o'clock and wandered towards the Liebestraum Hotel. The day sparkled bright and beautiful. Squinting into the light and then shading her eyes with her hand, she remembered Klaus' rude words of the last night. She wondered just how young this American was. She knew her face looked more aged in the sunlight. Maybe she ought to wear a sunhat so her face was shaded. But it was too late now, since she already had stepped into the entrance of the hotel.

Franz stepped out of his office as he saw the comely Renata approach the desk. Smiling, he offered her a good morning and accepted the envelope she handed him. No one else seemed to be around in the empty lobby, so there wasn't any need for any subterfuge in their transaction.

Renata leaned over the desk and near to Franz's ear. "Peter MacAllister," she said quietly. "Is he here?"

"He does have a reservation here, but we don't expect him until the afternoon train from Munich arrives. That would be after three o'clock." Franz gave Renata a broad wink. "Somehow I expect to see you again today," he said conspiratorially.

Peter stepped off the train and hailed a cab all in his first five minutes in Salzburg. He knew it was not a large city, and that the truly interesting and beautiful places were all clustered in a small area along the Salzach River. Actually, he was delighted to be asked by Arthur to make the trip. He felt confident he could make contact with their agent for the "stay-behind" army business. What he felt less confident about was his cover as a salesman for American high-end furniture. He and Arthur had racked their brains for a plausible kind of business he could pretend to promote here in Salzburg. They certainly knew he couldn't be a salt salesman. Salzburg meant salt castle. The Hapsburgs had built their fortune from the salt mines in the mountains several miles to the northeast of the city. No, bringing salt here would be like bringing coals to Newcastle or onions to Vidalia. So trying to push furniture would be his cover. His alternate story would be that he was a refrigeration salesman. That way, he could have a reason to approach several types of establishments, including restaurants. In fact, tonight he would try to make his first contact at a small, off-the-beaten-track place called "Die Heimat". First though, he would check into the Liebestraum Hotel.

Just as the bells were ringing their last peals a little after six o'clock that evening, Renata left her house and entered the flow of foot traffic moving towards the center of town. As usual, her presence caused a small stir of excitement among her faithful admirers. Tonight, though, their number was fewer because of the gentle drizzle that had begun in the late afternoon and was now making the cobblestones shine with the streetlights' reflection. By the time she reached the Liebestraum, her followers' attention had waned, and she could enter without any fuss. As she shook the drops of rain from the umbrella, she looked around to see if there was a young man in the lobby who appeared to be an American. Since no one there fit that description, she approached Franz, who had extended his shift at the desk so he could give Renata the information she needed about Peter MacAllister.

"Good evening, Fraulein Friedhof." Franz addressed her deferentially and formally for the sake of the guests who were milling around in the lobby.

"Good evening, Herr Zeller. And how are you this evening?" responded Renata with the same formality.

"Very well, thank you. The guest, whom you came here to meet, said you could find him at the Die Heimat restaurant. He asked for directions, and I told him he could find it around the corner and down five blocks on the right side of the street. He's a lucky man to have your gracious company this evening. He just left, so if you hurry, you can catch up with him."

Renata smiled and waved as she turned to follow her prey. She hadn't gotten a description of this MacAllister, but she figured that Die Heimat was a small establishment, and it would be a rare coincidence if there were more than one young American dining there tonight.

Peter had no umbrella, so it surprised him when one appeared above his head as he trudged down the street with the brim of his hat pulled down and his collar drawn up. Looking over at his benefactor gratefully, his eyes widened in surprise upon seeing a beautiful woman. She was giving him a dazzling smile, leaving no doubt that she found him attractive.

"You look like a man in need of some drying out. Our Austrian weather is unpredictable and can catch any of us unawares," said Renata as an explanation for her forwardness.

"Well, you sure came along at the right time, but I'm not going far—only two more blocks if the man at the desk in the Liebestraum is correct."

"Oh, are you going for dinner at Die Heimat? It has an excellent reputation for authentic, local cuisine. Tourists never find it, which is okay because it's a very small place. I'm going there myself since I got off of work early and don't want to cook for myself tonight." Renata wanted to make it clear that she was alone for the evening. She hoped he would ask her to join him at his table.

Upon entering the small, dim restaurant, they saw a short,

elderly and balding man in lederhosen hurrying towards them. He smiled up at them encouragingly and gave a welcoming bow and then led them to a table in front of the fire. Near to the fireplace and the table sprawled a large, black dog. He didn't move at their approach—only lifted his head lazily and gazed at them momentarily before laying his head down again with a sigh.

Renata smiled up at Peter as she sat in the chair he graciously offered. "I think the proprietor supposes we're together. Do you mind?"

"Of course not! I count myself a very fortunate fellow having your company for dinner. Since I'm new to Salzburg, I'm going to bombard you with questions about the area. Are you a native of the city?"

"Yes, my family has been here for three generations. We lived through the many changes that came with the German occupation, and then after the war, the Russians and finally the Allied occupation. Now we're so happy to be free—to be Austrian!"

Just then the little man came back to their table. With an engaging smile, he introduced himself. "My name is Herr Donner. My wife, the cook, and I are pleased to serve you this evening. We specialize in local Salzburger cuisine. Tonight we recommend our *bierfleisch* with a stein of *dunkles hefeweizen* to drink. The *hefeweizen* is one of our local beers for which we are famous."

Peter looked at Renata. "What do you think? After all, you're the native who knows what the best dishes are here."

"The *bierfleisch* is very much a traditional dish, like a casserole, and I highly recommend it."

With that settled, Herr Donner nodded, bowed and returned to the kitchen. Once the swinging door had closed behind him, he leaned over close to his wife, who was stirring the soup on the stove. Whispering, he said, "The man who just came in talks English like an American. He may be the contact we are waiting for. But the woman who's with him—I've seen her more than once with Klaus Habermeier, whom we know is working for the Soviets." Scratching his head, he mused, "How can this American, if he is the CIA contact, have been so easily snagged by a Soviet agent?"

His wife just looked at him and frowned. "Be careful," she counseled.

Back at the table, Renata studied the man across from her. He was certainly young and refreshingly friendly. She had found most Americans relaxed and less formal than Austrians— especially when they traveled alone. He smiled so easily and had small laugh lines at the corner of his gray eyes.

Peter was sizing up his tablemate also. The soft light of the fire played attractively across her face. She was certainly very lovely and slightly exotic to him in her Austrian dress. The confident way she held herself and displayed her charms, however, as well as the tenor of her voice made him think she was older than she looked.

Just then the black dog's limbs started to tremble, and his breathing became louder and sporadic. Peter grinned and reached down to pet the animal. "Good old boy! You must be dreaming that you're chasing a rabbit or a couple of squirrels. Now carry on, Fido. You're sure to catch them!"

Renata warmed even more to this young man. Maybe he had a dog as a pet. Her emotions were conflicted. She couldn't decide if she felt motherly or romantic towards him.

After Herr Donner had brought the *bierfleisch* in steaming bowls to their table, Peter asked Renata about Salzburg and what was it that brought so many tourists here. Renata became quite animated while talking about the music, especially Mozart's, and the puppets. She explained how the architecture of its most attractive buildings was influenced by Italy, where many of its archbishop princes had studied. And, of course, there was the fabulous natural beauty surrounding the city.

"What about furniture? There must be some that's locally made. Do they use wood from the surrounding forests?"

Renata shook her head. "That's something I don't know. Why do you ask?"

"Well, I'm a representative of an American furniture company, so I'd like to know more about my competition. Still, if the market isn't good for furniture, I also represent another company which sells refrigeration equipment. But I don't expect you know anything about that," Peter said with a wry smile.

Just then Herr Donner, who had been unobtrusively listening at the door, shuffled over to their table and approached Peter. "With your permission, sir, I couldn't help hearing that you know something about refrigerators. If you would be so kind as to step into our kitchen for a moment, I just want to show you that we have a problem with our freezer. Maybe you could tell us if we need a new one. I don't want to trouble you, but it would be so helpful to us, and it would only take a minute."

Peter, seeing the consternation on the old man's face, put down his napkin and, excusing himself to Renata, he followed Herr Donner to the kitchen. Upon entering, he was greeted by an old lady, whose face was wreathed in a large smile. She curtsied and wiped her fingers on her apron before offering her hand to him. Because of the old-world atmosphere of the restaurant, he hesitated, not sure if he was supposed to kiss her hand or shake it. Deciding to be gallant, he kissed it, which made her face crinkle into an even wider smile.

Leading Peter towards the freezer, Herr Donner talked loudly about how the compressor was unreliable—going on and off unexpectedly. Then reaching into the freezer, he turned the knob so that the compressor started with a whirring noise. Putting his mouth next to Peter's ear, he said, "October 25, 1955; the day we started to revive." It was a reference to the time of the evacuation of Soviet troops from Austria.

Peter didn't look surprised. It was the signal he had

anticipated and the reason he'd chosen this restaurant tonight. In response he said, "The Marshall Plan saved a lot of Western European countries."

Then the old man thumped Peter emphatically on his chest with his forefinger. "Why are you with that woman? She may be a Soviet spy. How can we talk with her around?"

"I know she's probably trying to find out what I'm up to, but the best way to deal with her is to show her that I've nothing to hide. How about if I come back later tonight after you close— say about eleven? We can talk then."

When Peter returned to the table, he assured Renata that indeed the freezer was malfunctioning. "I'm going to bring him my catalog later so we can discuss freezers. Who knows, this may be my first sale in Salzburg. What luck that we ate here tonight!"

Renata raised her glass in a toast. "Congratulations Peter! May you find many more malfunctioning compressors. It's a city full of restaurants, so there are endless possibilities."

Peter chuckled and, reaching over the table, clinked his glass to hers. "And now for dessert. What do you recommend?"

"Why not *Salzburger nockerl*? It's the perfect end to a lovely meal and to superb company."

Later that night, both Renata and Peter had unfinished business to do. Renata had to report to Klaus about what she'd learned, and Peter needed to get back to Die Heimat.

When he approached the restaurant with his catalog of refrigeration equipment under his arm, he was practicing his spiel as if he were really a salesman. Just in case he was being followed, it was best to keep in character.

Herr Donner was sitting at a table near the door working on tallying up the evening's expenses and receipts. It hadn't been a great night on account of the rain. After he let Peter in, he directed him to the kitchen where Frau Donner was cleaning up and making lots of noise banging the pots and pans. Anyone could tell there was no quiet intrigue going on here.

"Now we can talk business," said the old proprietor, motioning to a table with two utilitarian chairs nearby. "Show me your best freezer and explain why I ought to buy it instead of a European model."

Peter opened the catalog to a page that had a map of the Salzburg area tucked into it. Tracing his finger over the map, he asked, "Where do you think you have a problem now?"

Herr Donner adjusted his glasses over his nose, peered closely at the map and jabbed his forefinger in the valley between two nearby mountains. "There."

"Oh yes, the compressor. Well, it's proven that this model's compressor is not prone to the same problems as your European models."

Putting his glasses back in his shirt pocket, Donner stretched and sat upright. "I thought I overheard you say you also represent a furniture company. You know, we have locally-made furniture. Some of the wood used to make it comes from this forest."

"Yes, we do have a fine line of restaurant furniture. I didn't bring that catalog here tonight, but we can discuss what you need. You say the wood is harvested here in a local forest?" While Peter said this, he eyed the map again.

"Most of the harvesting is already done, but the stumps are left behind, so they are being removed by dynamiting. That leaves large holes behind in the forest. It takes a while to fill them in. I know the boys who do the work. It's in a very secluded part of the forest, but still not far from the city."

Now Peter knew how the weapons were going to be hidden. He also knew that Herr Donner was a valuable contact. Yawning in a satisfied way, he thought Arthur would be pleased with the news that the operation in Salzburg was working according to plan.

Renata had returned to the cemetery gate, which was unlocked—Klaus' work. After walking to the middle of the silent quadrangle, she slid smoothly into the mausoleum.

"Well," said Klaus, almost trembling with anticipation. Finally, he thought, we know who the CIA contact is here in Salzburg.

"Well," replied Renata while letting her shoulders slump as in resignation. "Peter MacAllister is no CIA agent. He's probably not even a good sales rep. I never had such a boring time as this evening at dinner with him. Can you believe it? He tried to induce me to spend the rest of the night with him. I wouldn't be able to bear it!"

Klaus looked at Renata with awe. He didn't think it possible for her to resist a young, handsome man. It felt good to know that even guys like that could be turned away. It wasn't as if he were the only one who was spurned by her.

Later, as Renata walked down the damp cobblestones and drew near her house, she laughed lightly under her breath and patted her hair. How good it felt to thwart Klaus and the Soviets. Peter had been a delightful dinner companion. And yes, he probably was with the CIA. Certainly he treated her as a woman longs to be treated by a man. Best of all, no references to age slipped from his tongue. He was not a loser like Klaus!

Chapter Nineteen

Luxembourg City

Time was of the essence. Now that Gilmary had made contact with the Soviet spy-master, she needed to move the action forward. No one had alerted her yet about whether all of the armaments had been stashed away in their hiding places. That the spy-master knew who she was and what role she would play in the communist's plans meant she must plot out her every action before it happened. Like an ant under a microscope, whatever she did would be magnified, watched and calculated.

After dinner that evening, Gilmary told Maria Goretti the pantry was out of canned vegetables, so she would get some out of the cellar. Clambering down the stone steps, she entered the food storage room and closed the door. The von Hollenden house foundations were quite ancient, and it was plainly visible here in the cool storage room. Large stones had been carefully fitted together in and around some naturally occurring rock. She knew this section of the old home stood above a part of the old Casemates. Because of that, it made her glad that back in 1867, when they had decided to destroy some of the caverns, they hadn't dynamited them. If that had happened, she'd be standing in rubble instead of their fruit and vegetable cellar.

The last time she had been down here, she'd been with Peter. It was then he had installed a secret telephone so they could communicate on a safe line. He knew the von Hollenden's regular phone line was tapped; he had tapped it himself so that the

CIA could monitor calls coming into the residence. Eventually, he figured the communist agents would also put a tap on it. He wondered what they would think when they saw the previous tap.

Now Gilmary moved a couple of large metal cylinders containing flour and reached for the telephone hidden in a shallow crevice in the foundation. In the dim light, she could just make out the encased wiring snaking from the phone, up along the crack between stones and towards the rafters.

Dialing the number she'd been given, she felt relief when Peter answered on the fifth ring, although he said nothing—just made a clicking noise with his tongue. Trying to keep her excitement in check, she took a deep breath and said, "We went to a baseball game recently and we actually thought we knew what the coach's signals meant. It was so much fun that we're planning on going again this weekend. We hope you can join us." With her message delivered, she hung up.

After reviewing in her mind what she'd just said, Gilmary shook her head, satisfied she had made the message clear. Peter had told her a positive message meant she'd made contact with the Soviets. A negative message meant no contact, and a positive/negative meant there was trouble. Now she would have to wait for more information and instructions.

Sunday morning found Gilmary sliding into a pew at Mass with Sister Maria Goretti and two dozen Polish workers, as well as a half dozen Italians. Over an aisle and in the second to the last pew sat a blonde woman, stylishly turned-out and wearing the latest Odette Millon dress sandals. While her eyes zeroed in on her prey, a satisfied expression formed around her lips. It would be easy to annihilate the young nun whenever she chose, because now she knew her workplace and the church where she could be found. Nevertheless, Olga figured she had to plan carefully—no slip-ups, and especially she didn't want to be captured again and sent back to Sardinia.

The last blessing was given, and Mass was over. The Polish and Italian workers were waiting for Maria Goretti to direct them to the hall where they could socialize and play sheepshead.

"Don't you want to learn to play sheepshead, Gilmary?" asked Maria Goretti as she looked questioningly at her friend. Maria Goretti was concerned that Gilmary felt excluded now the Polish apostolate was in full swing and taking so much of her time.

Gilmary just smiled as she looked into the concerned, blue eyes. Actually, she was happy Maria Goretti had found something so fulfilling to do while visiting. She'd been afraid her friend would be bored and intimidated by the constant need to speak French or Luxembourgish. But no, here was a creative spirit who had found an outlet for her energies. Thank goodness for card games!

Putting her gloved hand on her friend's shoulder, Gilmary urged her to join her new friends. "I would love to learn the game someday, but you go on ahead now. Besides, I'm not a fan of pickled herring and onions, and I know you'll all be having that with your beer."

She continued, "Tilly, the guide, and I have plans for the afternoon. She's going to drive me out into the countryside to visit her folks. So you see we'll both have a pleasant afternoon. I'll see you back home by 4:30 or so."

Chapter Twenty

Tilly was a natural tour guide. She enjoyed nothing more than pointing out the wonders of her small duchy. She knew its history well, having lived through its recent upheaval during World War II. Out in the village of Olingen, her parents had even longer memories. "It's a long road to Tipperary, it's a long way to go. It's a long road to Tipperary, to the sweetest girl I know!" sang Mr. Lanser with gusto in their living room. His wife watched him with amusement. She knew it was the only English he could speak, so he was regaling the young nun with his best rendition of the hit song of soldiers during World War I. However, if Madame Lanser had thought more about that earlier time and the devastation she and her countrymen endured in 1917, her mood would have darkened.

Today, though, was a fine day. Their daughter, Tilly, was here for lunch with her friend—a lovely, young woman from America. Her green eyes were lively and she smiled easily. Right now her husband, she thought, was just showing off. This young nun was fluent in Luxembourgish, so there was no need for Tilly to translate. They could talk about the news from Luxembourg City without awkward pauses while words were translated.

Two hours later, as the sun sunk lower in the western sky, Tilly and Gilmary bade the older couple good-bye. After hugs were exchanged all around, Gilmary tucked into her purse the recipe for *judd mat gaardebounen*, which had been the highlight of a delicious Sunday dinner. Then she and Milly drove off towards the city.

About five kilometers before reaching the outskirts of the city, they approached the entrance to the American cemetery. It looked impressive.

"This is a sacred place," explained Tilly in a reverential tone of voice. "It's here that over five thousand of your fine American boys are buried. They all died during the Battle of the Bulge or on the advance of their army towards the Rhine River. Far from home, they lie under the soil of a land that they died to liberate. We Luxembourgers are eternally grateful for their sacrifice."

Gilmary nodded in agreement, but had mental reservations about the secret Soviet agents existing in the shadows of this and every western European country. They weren't grateful to the Americans. Of course, these agents probably didn't consider themselves as Luxembourgers either. They felt a part of a larger identity—communist socialism.

Upon drawing up to the gate, Tilly suddenly looked crestfallen. She had wanted to show her friend the well-kept cemetery with its rows of simple, white gravestones. A large sign attached to the grill of the closed gate, however, announced the cemetery would be closed to visitors while renovations were being made. Getting out of the car, she motioned Gilmary to join her at the gate.

"How terrible! I wanted so much to show you this cemetery. It's something everyone should see—especially Americans."

Gilmary first looked sympathetically at her companion and nodded in agreement. Then she turned to look into the cemetery and the mounds of dirt and bushes blocking the view.

Suddenly, both women heard some faint noises, followed by wracking sobs. A small voice said, "Iggy, please don't."

Tilly's ears perked up. She grabbed the wrought iron

bars of the gate and called, "Ignacio? Is that you?"

The sobbing stopped abruptly, and all was quiet. Then the bushes moved almost imperceptibly, and two dark eyes peered at them through the foliage.

"Ignacio," Tilly tried again. Silence.

Finally, a weak but emphatic "No". "It's Renzo, Mademoiselle Lanser." Since Tilly was his teacher, he spoke very deferentially.

"Renzo! What are you doing here? You're a long way from home. What will your father think?"

At that thought, Renzo started to sniffle. Slowly he withdrew his head further into the bushes, and the two women heard renewed sobs. Then another's plaintive cries joined Renzo's. These new cries grew in intensity until Gilmary and Tilly became alarmed.

"Stop the noise!" Tilly ordered in her firmest, clarion voice that she used in the classroom. But her brow furrowed as she ordered Renzo out from behind the bushes.

When he crawled out and stood sheepishly before them, Tilly gasped. He was covered in mud and had scratches on his hands and face that were starting to swell into angry welts. Grabbing the ornate metal bars of the gate separating them, Tilly prepared to blast a lecture at him. She had plenty of ammunition.

Gradually however, she relented as she saw two large tears course down the dirty cheeks of the small boy. The stiffness in her shoulders relaxed as her natural empathy grew. Instead of scolding Renzo, she felt like dropping him into a warm bubble bath. Certainly, he would need one before his parents saw him again.

Gilmary meanwhile had been examining the gate and fence near the entrance. There had to be a way in since Renzo and his friend were inside. She found the gate, however, was closed and securely padlocked. The stone wall came right up to the gate, so there wasn't any space between them. Maybe the boys had climbed the gate, she reasoned. Standing back, she took its measure. It must be twelve feet high, she thought, too high for her to climb.

Turning to Tilly, who had crouched down and was trying to comfort the frightened Renzo, Gilmary wondered about the other boy—the elusive Iggy. "Where's your friend, Renzo?"

Renzo look up at the strange young woman. Then his eyes lifted questioningly to Tilly.

Tilly rose from her crouching position and stepped next to Gilmary. With a flourish of her hand, she said, "This is my friend, Sister Gilmary, Renzo. And yes, where's Iggy? We heard him crying. Is he as dirty as you are?"

Recalling his friend, Renzo became more agitated. He twisted around and pointed to somewhere past the bushes. "He's... he's way over there."

"Well, go and bring him here so we can figure out how to get you both out of there and back home," ordered Milly, who now felt responsible for her two students.

"I can't," lamented Renzo.

"What do you mean, you can't?"

"Well, he's stuck and I've tried to dig him out, but the mud just keeps falling in on him."

"Is he in a hole?" Gilmary could picture the child as having fallen into a collapsed grave.

"Yes, he's in a deep hole and he's scared!"

Tilly and Gilmary looked at each other with alarm. Since they couldn't see the hole, which must be behind the bushes, they imagined the little boy, Iggy, as buried alive.

"Ignacio, Iggy, can you hear me? Tell me that you can hear me!" yelled Milly, her voice betraying her panic.

"Si, Mademoiselle," a high-pitched, tremulous response called out. "I'm here, but I can't get out. Will you help me?"

Frantically, Tilly began to run along the perimeter of the wall looking for an opening.

Gilmary, staying at the gate, knelt down and quietly asked Renzo how he and Iggy had gotten inside of the cemetery.

"Away back there." Renzo turned and pointed vaguely towards one side of the cemetery. "We climbed up and into the bucket. Then we jumped down onto a big mound of dirt. It was easy," he said with a touch of swagger.

"Did you ever think of how you were going to get out again?" asked Gilmary.

Uneasily, Renzo dropped his gaze as the swagger disappeared. "No," he said weakly.

Gilmary realized that thinking through one's course of action was not usual for a seven- year-old. With a deep sigh, she asked Renzo to trot along inside the wall and shout when he got to the spot where they had entered. Quickly she got Tilly's attention, and the two of them ran along the outside of the wall, following Renzo's shouts.

Upon turning the corner, they spied the excavator with its arm and bucket straddling the wall.
"Now what'll we do?" asked Tilly.

"Maybe we should go back to the city and get the police, Tilly," said Gilmary.

But Tilly had already climbed up into the machine's cab. Looking down at her friend, she dangled two keys on a chain. They made a jingling noise as she jerked them back into the cab.

"What the...?" exclaimed Gilmary.

"How about that? The workman was so sure no one would play around with his machine, or he was just forgetful," Tilly said as she started the ignition.

The excavator's engine roared alive as exhaust fumes enveloped Gilmary. Coughing, she took shelter against the wall as the metal arm and its bucket began to swing up and over the wall. With a loud clank, the metal hit the top of the wall and scraped clumsily along its surface before dropping jerkily towards the ground outside of the cemetery. Then Tilly cut the engine and all was quiet.

"How was that?" she asked as she leaned out of the driver's window. Her face had a pleased, smug expression.

"You surprise me," cried Gilmary in awe. "Did you pay your way through college by working at construction sites?"

"No, but I'll try anything once. Now it's your turn. Hop into the bucket, and I'll lift you over the wall."

"No way friend! I'm not getting into that bucket and then smashing into the wall. There's got to be another way."

"Well, there's no other way, and you and I can do this. By the time we get the police here, Iggy could be buried alive. Just say a prayer. We don't have time for a novena!"

"Novena," laughed Gilmary dismissively. "In no time at all you'll have me in a grave on the other side, and I'm not a soldier so I'd be a dead interloper."

"So then," retorted Tilly, "at least I'm the only one who'd know, and I'm not telling!"

"That's only because you'd be responsible for my demise."

"Aw, come on. As you Americans say, 'It's all for a good cause,'" cried Tilly with bravado.

"How about if we trade places? You get into the bucket and I'll swing you over," offered Gilmary.

Tilly looked exasperated. "Don't you see, I'm not dressed for that. This is my new linen suit and the shoes are DiGiorgio's. My heels would get stuck in the muck. No, it's all up to you. Your shoes are low-heeled, and your suit is probably washable. So let's just do it!"

Throwing up her hands in defeat, Gilmary lifted her skirt and climbed into the bucket. Like a basketball player about to attempt a free throw, she crossed herself and kissed her thumb. "I'm ready," she shouted as she made her body small and compact down in the bucket.

Ponderously, the machine's bucket rose slowly into the

air. With the nun's weight, it didn't sway as wildly as it had before. Swinging it over the wall, Milly had to guess just how far down to drop it. She didn't want her friend to crash into a mound of dirt. Locking the arm into place, she cut the engine and listened.

Finally she heard Gilmary's voice. "I'm about three feet above the mound of dirt, so it's okay. I'll jump out now."

Scrambling over the dirt and grass, Gilmary followed Renzo. It was easy to know when they were near to Iggy; his shouts led them right to him.

Renzo dropped to his knees and motioned to Gilmary to look over the edge of the narrow, yet deep hole. Indeed, there was a small, wiggly mass of mud with a face above it staring up at them. No one in the world would have recognized Iggy. In response to seeing them, he began to wail.

"Hush! Hush, Iggy! Renzo and I are going to help you."

Looking around the construction site, Gilmary found several long planks of wood. After she and Renzo had dragged two of them over to the deep hole, she slid them carefully down the side and angled them so they resembled a slide. Returning to the construction materials, she grabbed some rope and an old piece of tarp. Once back at the hole, she tied one end of the rope to a tombstone and dropped the other end into the hole. "You grab the rope here, Renzo, and when I tell you to pull, pull as hard as you can. That way we can ease Iggy up the planks."

Iggy was already trying to pull his body out of the muck with the aid of the rope, but the suction of the mud wouldn't allow him any traction. Again he started to wail. Renzo joined in.

"Stop the noise!" yelled an exasperated Gilmary. "We're having an adventure. Enjoy it! Just think of the story you'll have to tell your friends."

Both boys became quiet and thoughtful. She was right. It was an adventure. They could imagine being the center of attention on the playground tomorrow.

Gilmary knew she'd have to slide down the planks on the tarp and haul Iggy out of the muck while Renzo guided him up the planks with the rope. Luckily, Renzo was a bigger boy than Iggy. She just hoped Renzo wouldn't topple into the hole with the rope.

After removing her shoes, hosiery and jacket, Gilmary looked ruefully at her clean blouse and navy blue skirt. Sighing, she wrapped the tarp around her skirt and slid down the planks. She was glad for the tarp because it slowed her slide and absorbed any wood splinters.

At the bottom of the hole, the mud oozed over her legs and up to her thighs. "Ouch," she said as her feet hit against something hard. Before she had solid footing, two small arms grabbed her at her waist and held on tightly. She smiled down at the little boy covered in mud. Gently she smoothed his matted hair. "It's okay now, Iggy. Renzo and I will get you out."

Then she lifted him onto the planks and giving him the rope, she looked up at Renzo. "Okay, Renzo. Pull him up, but take your time."

Renzo bit his lip as he pulled with all of his strength. He felt strong and heroic, but nevertheless, Iggy was a heavy weight.

Down below, the muddy little boy tried not to complain when his elbows and knees scraped the rough planks. "Keep on looking up at Renzo," Gilmary cautioned Iggy. "You're doing well!"

Turning around in the hole, Gilmary saw the end of several metal boxes protruding from the side of the hole. Wiping aside some mud, she read, "Ammunition". Another box was labeled "Rifles". How odd to have these in the ground of a cemetery. Suddenly it made sense. The cache of weapons! That must be the purpose of all of this excavation—to bury weapons.

Hermann Richter felt important. How better to spend his Sunday afternoon than with Comrade Herr Feldmeier. It was his chance to impress the communist spy master. After closing up his butcher shop, Hermann had hurried to pick him up in his new Audi sedan. Hoping to please Herr Feldmeier and to set the right atmosphere, he had Wagner's "Ride of the Valkyries" playing on the radio. Of course, he could have tried to find something by a Russian composer, but he felt Wagner set the heroic tone of their quest.

Herr Feldmeier was quite surprised at the choice of music. Did Herr Richter have a sense of humor, or merely a heightened sense of drama?

At their last meeting, Comrade Feldmeier had intimated that Hermann was just the right person to show him around the immediate countryside that surrounded Luxembourg City. He wanted to know where NATO was stashing their hidden weapons. He figured it would be close to an airport and a large population center. The Casements were the obvious place, but he wanted to rule out any other likely places.

Passing through small agricultural villages, they had arrived at the vineyard-covered slopes overlooking the Mosel River. After braking the Audi and then moving it off to the side of the road on the crest of one of the slopes overlooking the river, they both contemplated the sight of German soil just across the Mosel. Each man could envision how easily an invading army could cross the river and overpower this small nation. The Germans had done it in 1940, and the Soviets would do it again soon.

Hermann pointed out some caves on the lower flank of nearby hills on the Luxembourg side. "What do you think the odds are that caves like those are outfitted for hiding arms?"

Gazing at them reflectively, Feldmeier conceded, "It's certainly possible, but in order to deliver a large shipment of weapons, they'd need a road leading to the entrance. I think such a road would be a tell-tale sign of their intentions, and I see no such road."

Looking over at the beefy butcher, Comrade Feldmeier continued in a wheedling voice, "Come now Herr Richter. Think more creatively. Are there any old, abandoned factories near here? How about an abandoned steel mill or brewery?"

Hermann shook his head negatively. "I don't know about any such place, but we could send out a couple of our minor agents to search for disused factories and warehouses."

"Good. I'll leave it to you to do that and report back to me your findings in a couple of weeks. I have to make a report to Berlin soon about my recruitment efforts, and I can also include information about possible weapon caches. Now let's turn around and head back to the city."

So Hermann put the car in gear and turned away from the Mosel and towards Luxembourg City.

A half hour later, Comrade Feldmeier pointed ahead. "There's that American Cemetery we passed before. I wonder if they've filled all of graves, or if there's room for more. They may need them soon."

As the Audi approached the road that veered off towards the ornate gate, they noticed a car parked there and a lady in a green suit kneeling at the bars. She seemed to be shouting something, but to whom was not clear since the cemetery gate was closed.

"That's odd," observed Herr Richter. "What could she be doing there? She's too well-dressed to be kneeling on the ground. Maybe we ought to see what's happening." So he turned the car onto the access road.

Tilly had climbed down from the excavator and was back kneeling at the gate. She shouted to Gilmary, "What's happening there? Are you all okay? Just shout back to let me know you're all right."

"We're okay, or will be soon," came back Gilmary's

reply. "You'd better get back to your machine because we'll get to the bucket in a few minutes."

Tilly rose to her feet just as a silver car came to a stop next to hers. A beefy, middle-aged man with a red face and sparse hair climbed out of the driver's seat. The other passenger, who appeared to be another man, stayed put.

"Good afternoon, Madame. Are you in some trouble here? The cemetery seems to be closed." Hermann moved to the gate and read the sign. "Closed for construction, it says."

Tilly felt relief wash over her. Here was help, and in the form of a very strong man and his companion. Wonderful! After she explained the situation and Hermann had gone back to his car to tell Herr Feldmeier what was happening, both men accompanied Tilly around the wall and back to the excavator.

"Do either of you know how to operate this thing?" said Tilly hopefully.

Both men eyed the machine. Herr Feldmeier shook his head negatively, but Hermann climbed up into the cab and looked around at the controls. "I think I can do it. Let me practice."

With a roar, the engine came alive and exhaust once again filled the air. Hermann cranked the gear that lifted the boom and the stick and brought up the bucket. It jerked a couple of times, and then he let it down behind the wall again.

Now there were shouts from Gilmary. "Hey, Tilly, are you ready for us?"

"Yes," cried Tilly. "First send the two boys over in the bucket. We have help here now."

As Gilmary lifted the two youngsters into the bucket, she wondered who had come to their aid. Any help right now seemed welcome. "We're ready," she called "Up and over!"

Hermann then carefully set the boom and stick in motion. Slowly the bucket appeared with two frightened small faces peering over its side. After a somewhat bumpy landing, Tilly and Herr Feldmeier helped the boys up and over the side of the

121

bucket.

"Renzo and Iggy! Oh, don't touch me, dears. You're covered in mud, and this is my best suit. I'll hug you after your baths."

Instead of hugging Tilly then, both boys hugged each other and jumped up and down. Their fear had now turned to joy.

"Hey!" called Gilmary. "Don't forget about me! I'm still here, so send the bucket back over."

Soon the bucket was swinging back over with Gilmary gingerly holding her jacket, shoes and hosiery in one hand while the other hand steadied her in the swaying bucket.

Herr Feldmeier and Hermann noticed at the same time that they recognized the young woman climbing out of the bucket. It was their undercover agent. This was certainly perplexing.

When Gilmary saw Feldmeier, she stopped in her tracks and looked at him intently. Not knowing what to say, she stooped to wipe her mud-caked feet and legs with the hosiery. Those hose she could replace cheaper than the shoes.

Finally, she looked up to see Feldmeier's back as he retreated towards the car. But she had another shock when she saw the beefy man who was descending from the cab of the excavator. It was the man from the butcher shop! Why were both of them here together?

"Gilmary, we did it!" exclaimed Tilly. "Well, we did have a little help at the end, but basically we did it." She wanted to hug her friend, such was her elation, but she was mindful of her clothes, so she refrained.

Once they were standing next to Tilly's car, they confronted two new dilemmas: how would they take the boys home without ruining the car upholstery, and where would they clean up the boys before returning them to their parents.

Not to worry. Within the hour both happy boys were screeching in delight as they had a bubble-bath war in the von

Hollenden tub, and Nathan was busy cleaning out Tilly's car with a vacuum. Meanwhile, Tilly sat exhausted and rumpled in the kitchen drinking tea.

Back in Hermann's car, the spy master from Berlin switched off the radio and looked over at the other man. "What's going on here? Why is that agent turning up in such unexplained situations? I must get an explanation from her and soon! Do you think she recognized you? You said she'd been to your shop last week. It seems as if she's appearing in a variety of places and often. Let's hope she's not a free-lancing agent who will jeopardize our operation here."

Chapter Twenty-One

Luxembourg City

"It's already seven o'clock! Where's everyone? The train from Paris is always on time, so let's hurry up. We don't want to be late!" Nathan was pacing back and forth in front of the door that led to the garage. Every few seconds, he stopped, frowned and shouted out the time up the back staircase. Finally, he had results, as Gilmary and Maria Goretti clambered down the stairs.

"Do ya have to be so loud?" Gilmary asked scoldingly. "Mom and Peter are having a conversation in the library. You shouldn't disturb them."

"Yeah, what's that all about? Don't they want to come along with us and pick up Emile?"

"It doesn't take all of us to meet Emile. Besides, the car only seats four comfortably," reasoned Maria Goretti. Then looking more closely at Nathan, who was turning to go out of the door, she looked surprised. "Where did you get that Detroit Lions shirt?"

Nathan stopped, puffed out his chest for good effect and smiled proudly. "Peter," he said simply.

"Oh, my gosh! Some people do get spoiled. Pretty soon you'll forget that you're as much Luxembourgish as you are America," said his sister rather enviously.

Twenty minutes later, the trio stood at the train station observing all of the passengers who were exiting the train, which had just arrived from Paris. The noise of the crowd echoed off the walls of the lobby, creating an atmosphere of happy confusion. Nathan and Gilmary felt unsure about recognizing their cousin, Emile, instantly because he often sported an odd assortment of clothing. The only sure thing was that he would be distinctive in the crowd.

Standing on the tips of her toes and scanning the horizon over the heads of the crowd, Maria Goretti finally gave a yelp and started to wave. Hovering into view was a grinning face under a mop of curly, black hair and a battered top hat. When he got closer, Gilmary called out, "Emile, over here!"

At the sound of his name, he turned and started towards his cousins. Walking next to him was a petite, blonde young woman, whose gaze was riveted to a neon sign over the large clock on the lobby wall. The sign changed colors in waves of magenta, purple and orange. As Emile turned towards the little group that was welcoming him, the petite blonde kept moving straight ahead.

Suddenly, Emile stuck his hand out as if grabbing something, but his fingers came up empty. Then he turned towards the girl and ran after her while his cousins stood open-mouthed and watched him.

Placing himself immediately in front of the girl, he put both hands on her shoulders and gently stopped her. Then, taking his hands away from her shoulders, he began to make unusual signs in the air. She responded by signing back to him. The little group watching them began to suspect that the young woman was deaf.

When Emile turned and pointed to the trio, she turned and followed the direction of his gaze. Soon they were all shaking her hand as Emile made the introductions.

"This is Beata Lenski, a fellow student at the cooking

school. She's originally from Poland, but has lived in Paris for the last four years. As you can see, I'm learning Polish sign language from her."

Then turning to Beata, he pointed to Gilmary and signed an introduction. A broad smile spread across the Polish girl's pale face and crinkled the skin around her light blue eyes. She had the very white skin that Gilmary had noticed about the Polish bishop, Karol Konieczny, whom she had met in Rome. Then Emile introduced Maria Goretti and Nathan. Something he signed about Nathan emitted a reaction from the girl. She laughed a very natural chuckle. Finally, in a rather high, even voice, Beata said, "I very happy to meet you. I speak little English and want to learn more."

Nathan, his sister and Maria Goretti were surprised to hear her talk. Emile explained, "Beata didn't lose her hearing until she was eight years old, so she can talk, just not hear."

Gilmary looked at Emile quizzically. "You say you're learning sign language in Polish, but isn't sign language universal?"

Emile shook his head. "No, signing is specific to each language, unfortunately. The closest they come to a universal language is one called Gestuno. It's like the spoken universal language, Esperanto—hardly anyone uses it."

"Well, since you use your hands expressively anyway, it's a cinch you'll pick up the Polish signs easily," observed Maria Goretti. "Maybe I can learn some Polish signs too," she said with a wink.

Meanwhile, back at the von Hollenden residence, Peter was filling in Genevieve about his trip to Salzburg. Genevieve was especially interested to know if he had met the man who had tried to pass himself off to her as Jurgen Adler.

"No, but I'll bet the charming beauty who went out of her

way to meet me was one of his fellow agents. Actually, she was wonderful company—certainly better than your Jurgen impostor."

"Don't say 'my Jurgen'. I don't want to be linked in any way with that disagreeable man," she said with distaste. "But I am glad that you were able to make contact with the proprietor of the restaurant. So now, just what places do you want me to visit next?"

"Arthur's very pleased with your work in Norway and Sweden. The Salzburg connection was an unforeseen danger for you. Certainly, Arthur doesn't want to jeopardize your safety, so he's taking a break from making more contacts except for here in Luxembourg. Which brings up a small favor we are asking of you. We need you to host a bridge party on Saturday evening. You do play bridge, don't you?"

Genevieve waved a dismissive hand. "Of course. Who of my generation, especially if they were assigned to an embassy or consulate, doesn't play bridge? So who do you want me to invite?"

"Maria Goretti you already have, so how about inviting Tilly Lanser, the tour guide? Then you'll only have to find one other person." Suddenly Peter snapped his fingers as an inspiration hit him. Gilmary had told him that a banker and rose enthusiast named Dieter Braun was a low-level communist agent in the city. Maybe they could get one agent out of the picture for Saturday night.

"Are you familiar with a man named Dieter Braun? Is he a member of your rosarian society?"

"Yes, I know the man—not that I like him. But he does know his roses and comes to our meetings."

"We think he's an enemy agent, and it would help us if he were kept out of the action on Saturday evening. Would it be too much of an imposition if you invited him to play bridge?"

"And why a bridge party on that particular evening?"

Peter gave an exaggerated wink. "As Sherlock Holmes would say, 'The game's afoot!' You see, that evening's when we hope to finish off some important business, and it would be wise to make it look as if this house is lively. You know—lights and activity. Emile, your daughter and I will be occupied elsewhere."

Just then there was a racket at the door as Emile and the others returned from the station. Soon there were introductions and hugs all around, for any friend of Emile's was treated like family.

Chapter Twenty-Two

As Madame von Hollenden entered her kitchen through the swinging door from the dining room, she stopped to take a deep breath. "Ummmm, if the smells emanating from this kitchen are any sign of what you can do, I think the money spent by you two at the Chez Desiree Cooking School is a great investment."

Emile turned to smile at his aunt. He and Beata were in their element when whipping up an elaborate meal. They enjoyed working side-by-side and drew energy and inspiration from each other. Now reaching for a colander to drain the pasta, he marveled at the well-appointed kitchen. It certainly was the most modern part of the old house. Still, he could picture the first generation to use this place cooking their food in caldrons over a wood-burning fire. Now a large, modern gas stove and oven surrounded by colorful tiles occupied the original fireplace alcove.

Bubbling on the stove was a kettle of soup that Beata alternately stirred and tasted. Motioning to Emile to come and taste it too, and getting his nod of approval, she finally seemed satisfied and poured it into a tureen.

"Okay, folks! It's time to get seated, because the show's about to begin," crowed Emile.

As Gilmary sat in the chair Peter offered her, she was reminded of another banquet. That one had been last June at Villa della Fonte Fortuna near Rome. She and Emile were helping to cook and serve at a dinner for the members of the Christian Democrat Party that evening. The real purpose of her being there, however, had been to pretend to act as the assassin of the president of the Party, Aldo Falucci. She shivered at the memory. I'm glad there'll be no poisoning tonight, she thought.

Instead, this small banquet was in honor of Nathan's going away to America. Two days from now, he would be eating dinner with Peter's family in Ann Arbor. Grinning at the thought of all of the possibilities that would open up to him, Nathan pulled down his Detroit Lions cap and put the fork and knife upright in his hands on the table.

"Hey, brother! That's not good etiquette," chided his sister. "And what's with the cap? No one wears a cap in the house, and certainly not at the table!"

"It's my last act of rebellion in the Old World. I promise to be a model of good decorum when I reach the shores of the New World. If you'd like, I can have Peter's brother write a monthly report of my behavior—kind of like kindergarten. Besides, Emile gave me the cap and I want to show it off."

"That's right. I traded my chef's toque for that cap. A guy I know had it and was willing to trade. It's my last gift to Nathan until he comes home for Christmas."

After the fine meal was eaten, the family sat together in the living room before a blazing fire. Genevieve looked around the group pensively. What would her family look like in a few years? Her daughter, of course, was a religious, so she could never hope for grandchildren there. But Nathan—maybe he would return to the old family home someday with a wife and children. Then there were Emile and Beata. Certainly they made a great couple. Even though they had only been together a couple of months, they seemed very close. And Maria Goretti was like another daughter to her. She would be welcome anytime.

Finally, there remained Peter. Looking over at him, she felt perplexed. While not family in the way the others were, nevertheless, he was an integral part of their lives in so many ways. After all, soon her son would be taken in by his brother and parents in Michigan. That almost made them in-laws.

It occurred to her that she ought to make a trip in late summer or early fall to meet these generous people. Fall would be a good time to visit, she decided, because then Nathan would be starting college at the University of Michigan. In the meantime, she could scare up a few more native Luxembourgish roses. The pleasure she felt at that thought surprised her. She was beginning to enjoy her modest attempts at espionage.

Peter looked around the little group and marveled at how at home he felt here. In Rome he led a more solitary life and often traveled incognito to difficult spots where Arthur needed him to be. He enjoyed the challenge of having to think quickly and creatively in tricky situations, but here he could relax—at least until the weekend, when they would pull off their deception in the Petrusse Casemates.

Chapter Twenty-Three

Since Gilmary and Maria Goretti were gone from the house most of the day because they were working as scribes, Peter was free to come and go as he needed. Knowing it would be hazardous to walk about Luxembourg City looking like his normal self, he always disguised himself before venturing out.

Today, as the two nuns returned home for dinner, they were surprised to see a strange man turn into the gate before their house. He looked to be an older, distinguished gentleman, who walked with a limp. Upon reaching the front door and leaning his cane against the door jam, he extracted a key from his pocket and slid it into the lock.

Gilmary rushed up the steps to the porch and shouted, "Just a minute, sir! I think you have the wrong house."

As the man turned around he tipped his brown homburg to her in a courteous gesture then gave a shy smile and little bow. "I'm sorry Miss, but I think you are the mistaken one. You see, I am a guest here. Are you also a guest of this family?"

"No, I'm part of the family, and I don't remember seeing you here before. Did you just come today? How do you happen to have a key?" A perplexed Gilmary sensed that things were not as they seemed.

"Actually, the lady of the house gave me this key. She is a most charming woman." As the gentleman said this, he turned and opened the door. Then he stood back to let the two women enter first.

As Maria Goretti brushed past the unknown stranger, she looked him up and down. Something about his eyes looked familiar, she decided, but she couldn't remember where she had seen them before.

Upon closing the door after them, the gentleman put his cane in the umbrella stand near the door and laid his hat upon the entrance hall table. Then turning to the two nuns, he gave them a wide smile.

Why, he looks so much younger without his cane and hat! Gilmary thought. And the smile.... Why such a familiar, jaunty smile?

As he turned and led the way into the living room, both women were astonished to see him walking evenly and spritely instead of with an uneven limp.

"Ah ha," exclaimed Maria Goretti, as it dawned on her. "You are impersonating a character out of a Conan Doyle mystery, right? Could it be Watson or maybe Professor Challenger?"

As Peter sank into the sofa, he laughed. "Either of those characters could be my inspiration, but actually I'm Doctor Sigmund Metzler, professor of post-medieval European architecture. You'll be happy to know that I've just toured the Petrusse Casemates again in order to refresh my memory concerning their layout. They will figure in my chapter on fortresses of the north. There's some urgency in my present work, as my book publisher is hounding me to finish this part of the tome quickly."

Both nuns collapsed into another sofa facing him and laughed uproariously. "I think you have a future in the theater after you get too old for the espionage business," observed Maria Goretti. "Of course, you may be limited to Sherlock Holmes dramas, or maybe you could play Sigmund Freud. Was he the inspiration for your name?"

"Perhaps," replied Peter.

Later that evening, Peter followed Gilmary down into the cellars. She said they needed to restock the pantry after the meal Emile and Beata had prepared for Nathan's farewell, and he offered to help her.

As they descended the steps, Peter kept up some chatter about what he had observed that afternoon while promenading around the city. When they had walked further into the cellars and under the oldest part of the house, he motioned for Gilmary to come and look at something behind some shelves. It was an ancient, wooden door. Even though she had been a curious child, she had never ventured to open the door because it was locked, and she had been told the key for that door had been lost decades ago.

Now, however, Peter pushed the empty shelves aside, pulled a large, ancient iron key from his pocket, and fitted it into the lock. It swung open more easily than she would have expected. Pointing her flashlight at the hinges, she noticed traces of fresh oil lubricating the metal. "Your mother gave me the key," Peter acknowledged.

Gilmary looked astonished. "But my folks and grandparents always said the key was lost."

"They wouldn't have wanted you to go in here. Being you, you'd have gotten locked in or lost. I can't imagine what Nathan would have done if he had been able to enter these chambers."

As they shined both torches into the gloom, the light reflected dimly back at them from dark, rough stone surfaces. Gilmary realized they had to be standing above the Petrusse Casemates. As she had often thought, it was good that the parts of the two Casemates which were hallowed out below the city had not been dynamited. A whole, large section of the old city would have been reduced to rubble, and a great deal of their heritage would have been lost.

Following Peter, she slowed as he stopped and knelt down on the cold and slightly damp floor. Looking over his shoulder, she was amazed to see him lift a circular metal plate that looked like a manhole cover from the street and lay it aside. Two metal rings were sunk into its surface and allowed it to be lifted easily. Examining the underside by the light of her flashlight, she saw thick felt had been affixed to the metal plate so there would be no sound when it was moved.

Silently motioning Gilmary to follow him, he jumped five feet down into the opening. Lifting his arms, he helped Gilmary to slide down beside him. Moving the torch light back and forth, he silently showed her that they were in a very low tunnel which sloped downwards and into a larger space.

As both of them crept forward with their heads down because of the ceiling that became progressively lower, they noticed the freshening of the air. Just before the low tunnel from the cellar opening ended, their flashlights illuminated several wooden boxes piled in front of them. Upon closer inspection, they saw the words, "Ammunition" and "NATO" stamped on them. It astonished Gilmary to think of how close her family's home was to all of these explosives. She gave a shudder as she pictured her home blowing up if someone lit a torch to all of this.

Taking Gilmary's hand to guide her, Peter moved them forward and around the large crates. After walking twenty yards, they reached two large doors which were hung on huge hinges.

Putting his lips close to her ear, Peter whispered, "Outside of these doors are the Casemate tunnels—that is, those open to the public tour. As you may have noticed, numerous small holes puncture the inner walls of the caverns. In fact, there're so many, that after a while, no one pays any attention to them. Outside of these doors, however, there are four large metal rings which can be used to open this chamber. The hinges are kept well-oiled, so it won't be hard for you to put a thick rope through two of them and pull one of the doors open. Herr Feldmeier will willingly help you. The key to the lock on the doors is secreted in an aperture about seven feet off of the ground. The aperture is just to the left of the doors. Of course, the key isn't usually there, but tomorrow night, it'll be there by midnight.

"Tomorrow, you can take the tour of the Casemates, which your friend, Tilly, gives on the weekend. That way you can gauge how far you and Herr Feldmeier have to walk through the caverns to get to the recessed doors. Now I'll show you how this cavern leads into two other ones—all are filled with weapons in crates. Feldmeier can open any crate and find inside just what's marked on the outside of the box. Encourage him to open a couple of them so he feels certain of their contents. In fact, let him pick out which ones he wants to open. That should allay any suspicion he might have about you."

Taking Gilmary's hand and squeezing it, Peter continued. "I know you'll be nervous. He'll understand that too. But don't worry, because Emile and I will be hidden somewhere in these caverns and will come to your aid if it's necessary. I chose Emile to help because I don't want to include more people. The more who know about this, the less secure we are. Also, since he's living in the house, it's okay for him to know about the hidden entrance to these caverns. I wouldn't want anyone outside of the family to know. It might endanger the safety of all of you who live in the house."

Retracing their steps, they came back to the von Hollenden cellar and loaded some baskets with pantry supplies. Before climbing the steps to the kitchen, Peter quietly said to Gilmary, "Tomorrow evening, Tilly will arrive early and have supper with you before Dieter arrives. She'll have just come from locking up the Casemates, so she'll have the key on her. You must get the key out of her purse and before Dieter arrives you have to excuse yourself for the evening with the pretext of a migraine headache."

136

Gilmary understood how it would be dangerous for Dieter to connect her as a nun that he had espionage dealings with to Genevieve, as her daughter. She knew Peter had suggested that her mother remove any pictures of the family from the first floor rooms. Tonight Tilly would have to be warned not to mention that Genevieve even had a daughter. Beata would not be apt to bring up the topic, and Maria Goretti was already warned.

Chapter Twenty-Four

Dieter Braun distractedly rearranged the bills in the drawer under the counter. It didn't even bother him that one of the stacks stuck together. Smiling to himself, he felt quite happy that tomorrow evening he was invited to play bridge at Madame von Hollenden's home. He'd never been invited there before, even though they both belonged to the same rose society. Maybe Genevieve, as he thought fondly of her now, found him attractive. After all, he was available, and they both shared a passion for roses. In his own mind he already saw the two of them seated close together before a crackling fire in a cozy living room. She probably was moderately well-off, he speculated. It would seem so since she lived in a large brick and stone house near the overlook of the Petrusse Valley. Since his house was small and tucked away in a modest neighborhood, it made sense that he would move in with her after their marriage.

"Tap, tap." Someone was tapping on the marble counter-top in front of him. Looking up, he was shocked out of his reverie when he saw Frau Kolnberger looking reproachfully at him. The frown line between her eyebrows drew itself into a deep furrow, accentuating her dark disapproving eyes, and her lips were pursed, as if sucking on a cork.

"Guten tag, Herr Braun. I've been here a whole two minutes trying to get your attention. Here's my eight francs to add to my savings." Then abruptly sliding the money under the grill, she added, "Do you have any news about that rare 'rose of

the east'?"

Dieter coolly shook his head negatively. As of today, he felt superior to this small, frumpy comrade. He had been elevated to being an equal to the president of the Luxembourg Rosarian Society.

Gretta Kolnberger turned away from Dieter feeling that something had changed in their relationship. It unsettled her. At the exit, with one hand on the door, she looked up at the young person holding the door open for her. Why, it was a nun! Turning to watch the woman walk up to Dieter's cashier's cage, she ran into a man entering the bank. Brushing against him, she almost knocked the furled-up newspaper out of his pocket. He politely tipped his hat to her.

Because of these distractions, Gretta missed seeing a young blonde woman entering the bank just behind the man, so the older lady melted into the crowd on the sidewalk while failing to notice Olga.

Olga realized immediately that she had chosen an unfortunate time to visit Dieter Braun at the Freistadt Bank. Just now her nemesis, the doppelganger nun, was approaching his cashier's cage. If he looked up, he would recognize Olga and know there were two women trying to pass themselves off as the one Soviet spy.

Quickly, she grabbed the newspaper out of the man's pocket and flipped it open. Surprised, the man turned to look at this rude woman. But Olga, glancing his way, turned on a high-wattage smile and then trotted over to sit in a chair in front of a desk that was available for patrons' use. Keeping the newspaper held up before her face, she concentrated on filtering out the various voices. She hoped to overhear some of Dieter's conversation with the nun. Because there were competing conversations going on at the same time, it didn't work, so she casually left the bank a couple of minutes after Gilmary's departure. She would concentrate of following Dieter later when he left the bank for his break.

At exactly one o'clock, Dieter slid the wooden panel over the grill of his cashier's cage. Bidding his co-workers a good afternoon, he smartly placed his hat over his receding hairline and departed for the butcher's shop. He didn't mind visiting Herr Richter's shop; he actually enjoyed the conspiracy the two shared. Still, he felt he ought to be able to contact the Soviet agent from Berlin directly rather than having to relay all messages through Hermann. Just because Hermann was a German, didn't make him any better of a spy.

Nevertheless, Dieter obediently entered the shop permeated with the odor of raw meat and waited until all of the customers were served. Finally, Hermann locked the door, turned the sign around to read "closed" and pulled down the inner shade of the door. Together the men shambled into the back room.

Much to Dieter's surprise, Herr Feldmeier was seated at a table perusing a map of Luxembourg City. He looked up at the entrance of the two men, but didn't acknowledge them with a greeting or a nod.

Pointing to the map with his forefinger, he traced the outline of the Bock Casemates overlooking the Alzette River gorge. "This would be a perfect place to store caches of weapons, but I can't see how they could be gotten in surreptitiously and out again quickly."

Hermann moved to stand behind the Soviet agent and looked over his shoulder. "I can't think of how their army could do it either." Then leaning over and adjusting his bifocals, he pointed to another part of the map.

"You probably know there are two sections of the Casemates running through the city. There's that one running under the Bock Citadel and overlooking the Alzette River, but there's also the one running above the Petrusse Valley. It has numerous caverns and cannon apertures that are similar to the other Casemate. Both are open to the public for tours, so I can't see how they could also be used to hide anything." Then the butcher scratched his head and went to sit next to Herr Braun.

Feeling intimidated in the presence of the Soviet agent, Dieter tried to clear his throat so his voice would not come out as a squeak. With suppressed excitement, he finally addressed Herr Feldmeier. "Olga Diederich, dressed as a nun, came to see me today at the bank. She had a message for you. You see, she feels it's necessary to meet you and suggested tomorrow at noon at the Spanish Turret." Then looking at the map, he said, "If you permit me, I'll show you just where the Turret is located."

Sliding the map around to face Braun, the agent looked at him steadily. "Show me."

With a slightly shaky finger, Dieter pointed to a spot not far from the ancient cavalry barracks.

"Noon seems like a bad time to be meeting. Won't people be out walking the promenade then?" asked Feldmeier.

"Actually, it's out of the way for most people and too early for the workers who take a lunch break, so, no, you won't be noticed up there," observed Hermann. "Sometimes lovers go to meet in the turret, but they do that more in the late summer."

Feldmeier sat back in his chair, gave a sigh of resignation and said, "Okay, tell her when she returns to your bank for an answer, that I'll meet her there at noon tomorrow. Let's hope she has something important to tell me. We have to move this whole process along, as East Berlin is anxious for me to show them results. The recruitment of migrants into communist cells isn't working as easily as I had hoped, but if I can give them information about where the NATO caches of weapons are stored, they'll be so grateful that for now they'll overlook the lack of success in recruitment."

After Dieter left the meeting, he scurried along the Rue du Bonnet, anxious to get back to his cashier's cage in hopes that the young woman agent would come again soon for the answer from Herr Feldmeier. He felt gratified because of his importance in the chain of messages. There wasn't any doubt that he was a valuable member of the communist espionage apparatus. Suddenly, however, a new, troubling thought occurred to him. If the nun spy was now going to meet directly with Herr Feldmeier, maybe they wouldn't need him as their go-between anymore. Thinking about this new worry kept him busy until he entered his bank.

Chapter Twenty-Five

Gilmary walked along next to the parapet which led to the Spanish Turret. Deep below her in the Alzette River Valley was a magnificent panorama of blossoming trees and magnolia bushes.

Her mind alternated between admiring the view and imagining how deadly it would be to fall or be thrown off of this parapet and into the depths below. She fervently hoped the communist spy-master she was about to meet wouldn't have already ascertained that she wasn't a real agent. Otherwise, an unwary hiker below might come upon her body. Well, actually she was a real agent, just not as well-trained one, and certainly not a comrade.

Once she was abreast of the turret, she paused once more to admire the view, but also to turn and see if anyone was following her or was even near enough to notice her. Good! There wasn't anyone around, not even the spy-master, unless he was thin enough to hide behind a spindly tree. Swiftly trotting up the three steps that led into the shadows of the turret, she found the interior space was more confining than it appeared from outside. Basically, there was only enough room for one sentry. Now she wished the East Berliner would be thin enough to hide behind a spindly tree. She really didn't want to stand shoulder to shoulder with him.

Just after she had checked her watch and found it was five minutes past noon, suddenly, without a sound, there he was.

Dressed in a black overcoat and with a black fedora shading his eyes, he took up the little space that still existed in the tiny room. They were so close she could smell the licorice he must have sucked on recently.

"What news do you have for me?" asked Feldmeier without preamble. "Can you lead me to the weapons cache?"

"Yes, Herr Feldmeier, I can take you there Saturday evening, or more accurately, in the wee hours of Sunday morning."

The spy-master frowned. She shouldn't have addressed him by name when they were meeting in secret—that was an elementary principle of espionage. He wondered about her training. She seemed clever enough, but sloppy. Perhaps he should alert his superiors back in East Berlin that they must recall her for a refresher course. Now however, putting aside his doubts, he said, "Where are the caches?"

Gilmary stalled. "I can't tell you here, but if you meet me at midnight on Saturday at the corner of the cathedral, just before the promenade above the Petrusse Valley, I'll take you to them. If I say more, I may jeopardize the means of getting access to the hiding place."

Feldmeier now started to feel certain the hidden caches were in the Petrusse Casemates. The cathedral was just above that area of the city, so rather than pressing the woman for confirmation of his hunch, he just nodded assent and disappeared as suddenly as he had come.

Olga smiled to herself as she stood balanced on two stone outcrops that were part of the outside wall of the Spanish Turret. Balancing a couple of hundred feet above the valley floor didn't bother her a bit. Her mountain climbing skills and instincts were excellent. Since she had been thwarted in her quest for information about the meeting between the nun and the spy-master by following Dieter Braun to the butcher's shop, she had to follow Gilmary from her scribe's office. Yesterday she

144

thought she would be able to read Herr Braun's lips through the window as he gave her doppelganger's message to the butcher. It was unfortunate they went into the back room to conduct their business.

Now, however, she had heard enough to know when and where they were meeting. She too figured their ultimate goal was to get into the Casemates unseen and open the entrance to the cache of weapons. She would be there!

Chapter Twenty-Six

Genevieve looked patiently at Tilly, who was contemplating the cards in her right hand. Drumming the fingers of her left hand on the table, Tilly finally opened the bidding by announcing, "I bid one spade."

Genevieve immediately countered with, "My bid is two diamonds." Then she looked over at her partner, Maria Goretti, as if affirming her future bid. The young nun's face was screwed up in concentration and betrayed indecision.

Dieter Braun, the next bidder, was Tilly's partner, and was also dithering mentally, but finally said, "I bid two no trump."

Then Maria Goretti, who had only a smattering knowledge of bridge, studied her hand and saw that she had several diamonds. Rather tentatively she offered, "My bid is three diamonds." She then looked over at Madame von Hollenden for her approval, which was given with a smile.

Tilly continued the second round of bidding with, "I up the bid to four spades." Looking resigned, each of the other players sighed and passed. Now the real play could begin.

Next to Maria Goretti, wearing no veil tonight because she'd been told Herr Braun must not know she was a nun, sat Beata with a book about bridge balanced on her knees. Concentrating as she looked over the other young woman's shoulder, she felt glad that no one expected her to play such a complicated game. She wished Emile were here to sign to her what everyone was bidding, but he had told her Peter needed him tonight. She'd also been warned not to mention him or Peter or even Gilmary, so she just looked around and observed everything.

The little group had already been playing for almost an hour. Each one had a chance to be the dummy, and now that honor fell again to Dieter Braun. Carefully, he laid all of his cards on the table facing his partner, Tilly, with the spades on the left. Then he rose from his chair, sauntered over to the fireplace and leaned an elbow on the mantelpiece. He hoped his pose would remind any observer of a nobleman at ease in his manor house.

He rather liked being the dummy because he could get up and move around the well-appointed living room. Dreamily, he contemplated how he would enjoy living here with Madame von Hollenden. The two young blonde women were guests, he surmised, and Tilly Lanser was a friend of Genevieve's. That meant Genevieve lived here alone most of the time. Surely she must be lonely, but if he were here every evening they could regale each other with information about roses. He knew she had a car, so he pictured them motoring through the countryside and visiting all of the flower gardens in the duchy.

Hanging over the fireplace was an oil painting of the Mosel Valley. The golden frame surrounding the picture complemented the gold brocade of the drapes that hung on either side of the large windows. The proportions and appointments of the room were lovely, yet something about it struck him as strange. There were no photographs of family in the room— neither on the walls, nor in small frames on table tops. He knew she had a couple of children, although he didn't know if they were a son and daughter or even how old they might be. Maybe it was a good sign that there was no picture of her deceased husband. It would be easier for her to accept him as her new spouse.

Genevieve, having just played her queen of diamonds, sat

back and rubbed the muscles at the back of her neck. Looking over at Dieter, who appeared to be holding down the fireplace mantel with his weight on his right elbow, she wished the evening were further along. She couldn't wait to close the door on the bank teller so he could vanish into the night. His smirking smile and unctuous manner grated on her nerves. Thinking of him made her recall that other disagreeable man, the fake Jurgen Adler. Why was it, she pondered, that the secret agents she came across were duds? Apart from Arthur and Peter, she knew no suave and competent agents. Of course, she concluded, Arthur and Peter worked for the "good guys", while Dieter and the fake Jurgen, were the incompetents working for the Soviets. That served those communists right!

A loud "harrumph" brought Genevieve's attention back to the bridge game. Since it was Maria Goretti's turn to lead, she had cleared her throat, hoping that it would also clear her mind. Now she gazed pleadingly at Madame von Hollenden while slowly drawing a card from her hand and sliding it to the middle of the table. It was a queen of spades. Upon seeing it, Tilly was thrilled at Maria Goretti's blunder in leading trump because now she didn't have to fear an attack from the queen. Genevieve's face fell as Tilly, who had both the ace and the king of spades, played the king. A resigned Genevieve, having neither trump nor any other high card in her hand, failed off with the two of clubs. As suddenly as a kamikaze attack, the lead that she and Maria Goretti had built up instantly evaporated as Tilly took the trick with the ace of spades. Then the victor went in for the kill by quickly drawing trump, discarding her loser on her long heart suite and claiming the contract.

Wishing to bite her tongue, but unable to refrain herself, Genevieve said to Maria Goretti, "Why did you lead a spade, the suite that Tilly bid?"

Maria Goretti flushed and lightly hit herself upside her head. *"Dummkopf!"* she exclaimed. "I forgot about the queen not being the highest card."

Genevieve looked at her sympathetically while thinking that the young woman still didn't get it. Tilly, meanwhile, tried not to smile triumphantly as she enjoyed her moment of glory.

"This game's too complicated for me!" an exasperated Maria Goretti exclaimed. "I don't know if I'll ever understand it. Too bad, because I know a lot of intelligent people play it." Then with a brightening continence, Maria Goretti looked around the table and asked, "Who here knows how to play sheepshead? Now that's a game I understand."

Looking at Tilly and Madame von Hollenden as if to win them over, she said, "It's a game that gives value where it ought to be given—the queens are the high cards. Each queen is worth four points, but her real value is that she trumps all other cards, even the king."

Tilly nodded. "I like the concept, and yes, I do know how to play it. Most Luxembourgers, who live on farms or in small villages, play it with their neighbors. Even Herr Braun must know how to play."

From his perch near the fireplace, Dieter nodded an affirmative, although he felt that to play such a game was beneath himself and Madame von Hollenden.

Even Beata looked up and nudged Maria Goretti to write down what everyone else was talking about.

"Schafkopf," wrote Maria Goretti in German. Nodding her bright head, Beata beamed as she said in a pleasant, rather high voice, *"Tok, tok."*

Genevieve looked bewildered. Sheepshead was not a game one played at the embassy card parties. It was considered more of a tavern game—rather like drinking beer instead of champagne. But since she had forced Maria Goretti to play bridge, and because Beata would be included in the game, she acquiesced.

Soon it was Genevieve who was concentrating hard on

remembering rules and values of the cards. Maria Goretti, on the other hand, felt relaxed now and totally in her element. Instead of feeling like she was playing in a fancy drawing room, she imagined this was as informal as playing with the Poles in the back room of the Chez Maurice.

"I think," observed the young nun, "that having the queen as the most valuable trump shows an innate sense of proportion. Did you know that at one time the Poles couldn't agree on a man to be their king, so they appointed a woman, Jadwiga by name, but also known as Hedwig, and called her their king? King Jadwiga has a fine ring to it," she said with a dimpled smile.

The Place de la Constitution was bathed in an uneven pattern of light and dark. It came not from the moon—there was no visible moon tonight—only a dark sky with heavy, damp clouds rolling in from the west. No, the moist halo of light and shadow emanated from the ornate street lamps which formed a crescent around the esplanade overlooking the deep chasm and the river below that cleaved the city into two, uneven parts—the larger old city and its newer, younger sister.

Peter adjusted the collar of his trench coat up around his neck. Brrrr! It was damp and clammy here on the esplanade— certainly not the kind of night he'd have chosen for an evening stroll. He was not alone, however. At least a dozen couples— some young, some old, were promenading along the railing. The pattern of light from the street lamps undulated as the couples strolled in and out of the shadows.

Out of habit, he pulled out his briar pipe and stuck it in his mouth. Then he caught himself. Of course, he couldn't light it since the sweet smell of the tobacco would be a dead give-away of his presence. So he merely chewed thoughtfully on the stem and checked his watch. It was a quarter past midnight and soon the esplanade would be empty.

Just then he spied Gilmary with a man coming around the corner of the cathedral tower. The man was of average height and walked like an athlete—confidently and gracefully. Like Peter, his overcoat collar was turned up against the chill, and he wore a dark fedora pulled low over his face. Both of his hands were in his pockets, but occasionally he would pull one out in order to gesture with it, as if emphasizing a point of conversation.

After the man and the nun had walked to the edge of the esplanade and into the light of a street lamp, they paused to look over the chasm.

Leaning over, the man pointed into the gloom towards something below. Gilmary nodded in agreement, then casually turned her back to the chasm and leaned on the railing. As she did so, she nonchalantly adjusted the ends of her sleeves over her wrists and then touched her chin thoughtfully, as if contemplating some words of wisdom that her companion had just uttered.

Under the brim of his hat, Peter's eyes became alert. Looking towards Gilmary and the back of the man, Peter, with both hands, deliberately adjusted his hat both front and back. Then he turned and disappeared.

"Yes, I totally agree with you that the majority of people have no idea of how to govern themselves. They're worse than sheep—more like lemmings." While Gilmary was saying this, she was trying not to smile. In reality, she was thinking of the signs that had just passed between Peter and herself. Just like being on first base, she thought. But the difficult and dangerous part still lay ahead. She must yet run to second, steal third and slide into home.

In order to give Peter and Emile time to hide themselves in a cavern of the Casemates, she'd have to stall Feldmeier, who was her companion for this stroll. Turning back to him, she tried to pick up the thread of conversation. "My experience of dealing with these Italian migrants, who come to me for help in writing up business agreements or translating, is very instructive on how they think about themselves."

The Soviet agent turned and looked attentively at the young woman. He was not only interested in how the Italians thought, but also in how she would interpret it. "I'm quite interested in what you have to say because they've been difficult to organize into a communist cell here."

Gilmary pulled away from the railing and continued to walk away from the direction where Peter had disappeared. The older agent turned and joined her as she continued speaking.

"These men are mainly interested in finding jobs that pay enough for them to send some money home every month to their families. They work hard for long hours and often in dangerous situations. Since they're bone-tired in the evenings, they have little energy or interest in talking politics."

Feldmeier, clasping his hands lightly behind his back, responded, "Then we have to lure them on weekends and holidays to something they'll enjoy. Gradually they'll come to trust and follow us."

Gilmary nodded. "It will take time and ingenuity."

Suddenly Feldmeier stopped and looked around. The esplanade was almost deserted. "It's time we retraced our steps and got back to the entrance to the Casemates. Even though our conversation is instructive, the real reason for our evening stroll has to be attended to. I'm quite excited to see what you've found."

Standing in deep shadow and out of the pool of light bordering the esplanade, Olga looked out across the deep chasm and recollected that she had never explored the new section of the town. She'd been too busy trying to find her prey and develop a plan to get rid of her. After tonight though, she'd be free of her nemesis. Then she could work to reinstate herself in the good graces of the Communist Party.

Olga had anticipated this night for weeks and now she trembled slightly with nervous energy. Grasping the railing that ran the length of the esplanade, she peered down into the depths of the chasm. If she leaned outwards, the dark holes that distinguished the face of the rock wall beneath her were partially visible. They were some of the many apertures for cannons.

Earlier in the day, in strong sunlight she had examined the holes from the valley floor. Shading her eyes from the sun, she had viewed three likely entrances, for she intended to enter the Casemates through one of the apertures. Using a six inch ruler, she held it up in front of her, closed one eye and roughly gauged how far it was from the cannon hole in the stone wall to the esplanade above. Probably 100 feet, she reckoned—an easy climb. In fact, it was about the same distance as the cliff face at Capo di Marrargui near the prison in Sardinia. Thinking of that climb eight weeks ago, she chuckled. She'd done that one with those two dunces, Ivan and Uri. This time she was on her own and liked it that way.

Ten minutes later, the bell in the cathedral tower tolled once. It was an hour past midnight and the silent old part of town near the Place de la Constitution was deserted. A very light drizzle started to fall, but Olga was not concerned because her rope was still dry, as it had been wrapped carefully in an oiled burlap bag. Looking at her feet, she reasoned that her new climbing boots would do just fine on the rough stone wall below even if it became wet.

Taking out the rope, she tied one end expertly to the railing and carefully unwound the rest of the coil, dropping it until it dangled a few feet past the cannon aperture. Stepping over the railing, she wrapped the rope around her right hand and clamped her feet around the thick coil that dangled below. Slowly, hand over hand she descended into the gloomy chasm.

Chapter Twenty-Seven

Peter and Emile entered the cavern housing the NATO armaments through the low tunnel that began under the von Hollenden cellars. The final five feet of the opening were only three feet high, so they had to crawl out and enter behind the wooden crates filled with ammunition. Again, Peter noticed how the air became noticeably fresher upon entering the large cavern. On his last inspection during the public tour earlier that day, he had noticed a couple of recessed openings which were covered with a tight grillwork. They allowed air to circulate into the cavern and keep it drier than it would be naturally.

Carefully turning on their battery-run torches, covered now with a piece of thin fabric to soften the glow, the men made their way into an adjoining cavern further into the rock. It was also filled with crates of weapons. Beyond this second cavern, there was yet another one containing crates marked with NATO's stamp. After that, the walls were stone dead-ends. Taking up positions on opposite sides of the room, each man turned off his torch and settled in uncomfortably while waiting for Gilmary and Feldmeier.

Gilmary thought the stairs down to the first cavern were more numerous at night and in the dark than they had seemed during the day. Feeling their way with only the thinnest of light to break up the intense darkness, it took them a long time to

154

descend the ninety steps.

It now seemed the easiest part of the whole operation had been stealing the key out of Tilly's purse while she was still at the table during supper. Stealing from her friend made Gilmary uneasy, but she figured she could return the key in the afternoon before Tilly's first tour. Her lame excuse would be that she found it in the front hallway under the side-table. It must have fallen out of Tilly's purse and been accidently kicked under the table when she took off her overcoat.

Upon reaching the final step, the nun could feel her heart pounding in her breast. Surely it was pounding from exertion, but also from fear and excitement. Beside her, she could hear the heavy breathing of Herr Feldmeier. Apparently the descent had been an exertion for him too, even though he appeared to be in superb shape. Of course, he also had the added weight of a length of heavy rope he had retrieved from near the entrance to the Casemates. It would be needed to pull open one of the doors to the caverns containing the weapons by linking it through the iron rings.

Now turning to her right, Gilmary began the journey down the long, snaking tunnel until they could reach the end of the section that was open to the public. The Soviet agent followed without her having to signal the direction. Of course, he too must have taken the public tour at least once, so he would be familiar with the layout. Nevertheless, even if a neophyte thought they knew these tunnels, it was possible to get turned around, confused and lost. There were numerous openings along the main tunnel that veered off into secondary tunnels and caverns. It made sense that the total space of these caverns was enormous since thousands of Luxembourgers took refuge in them during the World War II bombardments.

It smelled too. Gilmary hadn't noticed the smell when she was here during the daytime. But at night the air was damp and slightly moldy. Because of that it was a relief every time they came to the loop-hole openings for the cannons. Then the air was less damp, and they could see for several feet in all directions because of the reflected light from the city.

Since they weren't sure if anyone could see lights in the loop-holes from across the valley, they kept their torches out until they were deeper into the tunnels and away from the openings. Feldmeier calculated it would take them at least twenty minutes to traverse the length of the tunnel. But that was in daylight. Tonight it probably would take twice that time.

Ten minutes into the walk, Gilmary stumbled and her left shoulder crashed hard into the sandstone wall. Feldmeier moved his torch so it would illuminate the woman, and saw her face was screwed up in pain. When he stepped closer to her, the nun could smell licorice again. Quickly she moved forward and carefully shined her torch on the path ahead, paying better attention to where she stepped.

Finally, there was an iron gate before them. It was kept locked so no one could enter the tunnels from the long, eighteen-foot wide ramp on the other side that led up to the street above. It had been built long ago by soldiers who needed a means of bringing cannon, wagons of armaments and other supplies into the Casemates—not to say their horses, too.

Gilmary figured Feldmeier would be wondering why they'd chosen such an arduous means of arriving here when they could have entered through the ramp just beyond the iron gate. Speaking softly, she informed him, "There was no way I could have gotten the key to this gate. It's never open for public tours, so no one knows who's in charge of the key." Then turning back and measuring out twenty paces, she retraced her steps until she came to a place in the sandstone wall where four large, iron rings were fixed into recesses in the wall. Shining her torch on them, she motioned for the Soviet agent to come closer.

Feldmeier gazed at the four iron rings with mounting excitement. When he had examined the tunnel during the public tour, he'd never noticed these rings. There were so many recesses in the walls that after a while, it seemed unnecessary to pay any attention to them. Turning to look at the agent he knew as Olga Diederich, he saw she had moved about ten feet away and was using her flashlight to carefully examine some smaller recesses high on the wall. Reaching up, she tried to put her hand on a small ledge, but was not tall enough.

"Herr Feldmeier, I need your help," she whispered. "The key for the lock on those doors is up here I think, but it's too high for me to reach."

After he had retrieved the large key, they moved together towards the formidable doors, unlocked one of them and threaded a length of rope through two of the iron rings. With some effort, the Soviet agent was able to move the door enough for them to sidle through a narrow opening.

Once they were inside, Feldmeier stood waving his torch around. Then in total amazement, he walked swiftly from one large crate to another. "Rifles, ammunition, howitzers," he said softly in awe. "It's all here, just as we had hoped!"

Gilmary felt the tension go out of her shoulders. She didn't realized how strained she had felt up until now. Assuredly, somewhere in these caverns, Peter and Emile were listening from their hiding places. That gave her a sense of not being alone with this dangerous man.

Moving further into the first cavern, the East Berliner suddenly tripped over a piece of metal in the shadows on the dark floor. Reaching down, he picked up a crowbar. Excitedly, he went to the nearest crate and, using the tool, he opened the lid of the box. Sure enough, there were rifles just as it was marked on the outside of the crate. Gilmary smiled to herself. It was almost too obvious that someone had left the crowbar there just so the agent could use it to discover for himself what was hidden in the caverns.

Speaking to himself in German, Feldmeier almost danced

from crate to crate, reading off in a muffled tone the items stored there. It was a real coup to be able to announce to his superiors in Berlin that he had found the "stay-behind" army's secret stash. Of course, he would probably tell them of the minimal help he had received from Olga Diederich. After all, she had led him to it. Nevertheless, already he had surmised that this was the most likely place for the weapons to be hidden. She had only confirmed his suspicion.

With her hands entwined in the rope, Olga's feet balanced easily against the wet, stone surface as she hung over the chasm just to the side of the loophole. The light drizzle had coated her black, tight clothing so it glistened softly in the reflected light from the city above. While keeping out of sight on the outside of the Casemate, yet she could see the feeble light of the flashlights of Herr Feldmeier and the young nun. They'd made slow progress. But now finally they appeared at the end of the tunnel's path and up against the iron-clad gate that blocked off the rest of the caverns.

She heard their murmurs as they searched for the key, set it in its lock and pulled on the heavy rings until the metal door had opened enough for them to enter. Waiting until their lights faded and their gentle rustling had subsided, she swung her body across the threshold of the cannon-less loophole and landed with a soft thud inside the Casemate.

Creeping towards the narrow opening of the large metal door, she halted when she reached it. Hesitantly, she peered into the gloomy cavern. All she could see was the faint movement of light far back in the formless space. Large, squared-off dark shapes blocked most of her view of the shifting lights.

"Ach, dies ist wunderbar! Phantastisch!" Olga heard the excitement in the low rumble of the German's voice. Her own excitement grew as she listened to him. This is the moment

I've waited and schemed for, she thought. It's all come together now. I'll expose the duplicity of the CIA mole and claim my rightful place again as the Stasi assassin. Oh, it'll be so good to operate within the organization of fellow comrades instead of having to figure everything out by myself.

Nevertheless, Olga waited near the door. Her training warned her to always have an escape ready, just in case she had miscalculated the danger.

Crouching in the darkness, she felt for the knife positioned in the small of her back. Then she checked the other smaller blade strapped to her right shin. In her pocket, she felt the outline of the garrote she always carried. Even though she hadn't used it recently, it was a part of her standard equipment, as was the pliable rope she carried so she could truss up her victim.

Now she moved just inside the door and close to the wall. Grasping the shank of her black metal flashlight in one hand, she carefully drew the small knife into the other hand.

Having assured himself that the large boxes all held weapons, Feldmeier started back towards the front of the first cavern and the door. As he advanced, he swung his torch back and forth in front of him. Elated, he stepped lightly past the enormous crates. What a find! What a coup!

Behind him, Gilmary moved ahead more hesitantly. She was trying to figure out their exit and how she'd be able to ditch the Soviet agent before going home. Certainly, she didn't want him to follow her and find out where she lived.

She remembered he'd kept the key that opened the large door in front of them which allowed access into these caverns. Belatedly, she felt she ought to have insisted on keeping it herself. Her insistence, however, might have raised his suspicion of her. No, it was better for him to take ownership of this plan. After all, he was the one who'd need to pass the false information on to East Berlin and Moscow.

Now they'd both entered the empty space of about

eighteen feet before the door to the cavern entrance. Gilmary figured the space was left empty so a forklift could maneuver the crates of weapons around without bumping into the walls.

Suddenly, a strong beam of light stopped them and pinned their feet to the floor. Startled, Feldmeier backed up three paces and turned sideways, while aiming his own torch towards the light. With his right hand in shadow, he reached into his pocket for his gun. The cold metal of the silencer was what his fingers encountered first as they curled around the barrel.

Gilmary's left arm came up to shield her eyes from the bright beam. Seeking the source of the light, she aimed her own flashlight so it played over the figure in black tights and turtleneck sweater. The woman's hair was covered with a tight, black knit cap. But it was the face that arrested her; it was her own face. The expression was more intense, but the arched eyebrows and curve of the jaw were the same. Staring back at her was the very same face that she had momentarily seen a year before in the Basilica of St. Peter in Rome. Olga Diederich! It had to be her. So she had escaped the Sardinian prison and survived the cold, wet journey in the Mediterranean!

But what was she doing here? The answer arising in Gilmary's mind made a cold, pin-pricking sensation crawl up her spine. Suddenly, she felt more danger from this woman than from the Soviet agent beside her.

Herr Feldmeier wanted to rub his eyes and clear his vision. The figure in black, who was confronting them with her own strong light, was the young agent who had accompanied him down here. But no, that agent was beside him, and she was wearing a dark blue trench coat, not black tights and turtleneck.

Quickly, he looked to his side to confirm his memory. Yes, she was still there, although now she was moving slowly away and off to the side a few paces.

Pointing his gun first at one and then at the other, he shouted, "Halt! Freeze!" Then training his beam on the

160

interloper in black tights, he demanded, "Who are you?"

Olga was only too eager to oblige him with the answer. "Olga Diederich, Comrade! I'm Olga Diederich, the Stasi assassin." Then, swinging her torch to envelop Gilmary in the strong light, she spat out contemptuously, "She's not a real communist agent! She's a CIA operative pretending to be me."

Gilmary was speechless. Nevertheless, the heightened danger of the situation prodded her to stammer, "Hilda. What are you doing here? Why do you always have to follow me around and pretend to be me?"

Olga's jaw dropped. What effrontery! To call her Hilda. It was madness! She wanted her own identity back.

Sputtering, Olga blurted out, "Don't believe her! Her whole act is one contorted lie."

Gilmary quickly cried out, "Can't you see we're sisters—twins? Only she always denies it. I'm the real communist agent; she just pretends. She's delusional. Our parents tried to get help for her, but she keeps escaping from the hospital."

"Hospital! No, it was a prison in Sardinia, and my parents didn't put me there. You did! You are the thief of my identity. I'll kill you to get it back!"

Now Olga was seething. She wanted to throw the knife she held in her slightly trembling hand and kill this lying creature. Feldmeier's gun was aimed at her however, so she'd have to wait to kill her doppelganger. Instead, now she'd have to win the debate against this evil CIA agent.

Feldmeier looked from one young woman to the other. With an exasperated groan, he thought how wrong it was to have women agents. He'd always considered them a liability, but sometimes one had to suffer having them as partners. But this was too much! Just when he had a great coup before him and wanted nothing more than to get this information to his superiors as soon as possible, he had a conundrum. Who were these women? Were they necessary? Would anyone care if he got rid of both of them? He'd suspected from the beginning that the agent disguised as a nun was a loose cannon.

Olga weighed the man's silence. The longer he kept quiet, the more anxious she became. This situation was not progressing as she had hoped. Slowly, she moved backwards, towards the door—her escape route.

Perceiving the receding beam from the flashlight of the interloper in black, Feldmeier aimed his pistol and fired towards the disappearing light. The silencer was effective, but the bullet made a pinging noise as it ricocheted off the metal door and hit the sandstone wall.

Gilmary froze in terror, but immediately a hand clamped over her mouth, and she was lifted off her feet and swung around behind a crate. In one dizzying, quick movement, she was slung over someone's shoulders and carried back into the cavern.

Comrade Feldmeier swiveled on his heel and aimed his pistol to where the nun had been standing. He fired even before he had time to train his torch's light on his prey. When he did get his torch aimed, he saw no one—just empty space where the woman had been standing.

Quickly, he turned and ran towards the spot where she'd been. Swinging his torch wildly back and forth down the line of crates, he searched for some sign of her. Nothing! Just an indistinct scraping noise could be heard coming from somewhere in the cavern.

With irritation, he considered that the woman in black, whom he had shot at first, was now getting away through the Casemates. Maybe he'd have a better chance of catching her as she fled down the tunnel.

Rushing to the door, he slid through the opening and ran to the left towards the long, yawning labyrinth. Directing his beam ahead, he saw an empty corridor. Running forward, he sprinted for half a minute down the path, stopping intermittently to listen for footsteps. He heard nothing; he saw no one.

Weighed with foreboding, Feldmeier turned back towards the caverns and retraced his steps. With relief, he saw that the crates of weapons, at least, had not disappeared. He hadn't just imagined them. He was also quite sure the woman in the trench coat couldn't have sneaked out either while he was pursuing the other agent. He had shot at her; she must be scared and still hiding in the warren of weapons crates. Well, there was one way to make sure that she, anyway, was never heard from again.

Taking the large key out of his pocket, he heaved the heavy door closed and locked it. With an evil smile, he pictured her dying alone and in agony from hunger and thirst. Well, he reasoned, if she were a real nun, her prayers would keep her company. Let the angels come and console her! Then he stood still and debated with himself whether he should replace the key in its hiding place or take it with him.

It was a dilemma. If he left it, the woman in black, who had disappeared into the Casemates, could return and steal it. But if he took the key, the NATO agent who must periodically check these caverns would know that someone had probably breached their hidden cache. Then they'd have reason to move the weapons, and he'd have to search for them all over again. Finally, he decided to leave it in its nearby niche. That looney woman, whom the other one had called Hilda, and who may have escaped from a mental hospital, would no doubt have been scared off by his shooting at her. Too bad he had missed!

Once again, Olga hung over the chasm outside of the loophole. Even though she was seething inside with frustration, she had enough discipline to hold herself quiet and listen to the sounds emanating from the Casemate. When she heard Feldmeier run away from the gate and down the tunnel, she began the climb up the face of the cliff towards the esplanade. Then she thought the better of it, so she went back down to listen and find out if her doppelganger had managed to escape the caverns. No one, however, except Feldmeier exited the cavern. As she strained to hold herself steady on the rope, she heard him shove the heavy door shut, lock it, and after a long pause, replace the key in its niche.

Just a few minutes ago, she'd felt in awe of the East Berliner. Now she only felt contempt for him. Before this moment, she'd only two scores to settle; the one with the nun; the other with Fritz Eichel. The finality of what had happened to her nemesis suddenly hit Olga. Her doppelganger was either dead inside the caverns or buried alive with the weapons. Setting her face into a look of grim determination, Olga resolved that going forward from here, there would be a third score to settle. Life had just gotten more complicated.

Gently laying Gilmary down at the foot of the opening that led up towards the von Hollenden cellars, Peter gave her a shove forward. Just inside the low, tight tunnel, Emile pulled at her arms, sliding her towards him. Soon the three of them were crawling upwards until they reached the point where they could stand up and hoist themselves into the cellar.

Standing now above the hole, Emile and Gilmary looked back down into the darkness. Peter had disappeared.

Emile whispered to his cousin, "He went back to find out what's happening to Feldmeier." Feeling her shaking and gauging how near she was to collapsing, he led her into the lighted part of the vegetable cellar. There he settled her on a crate of onions. Spying an old blanket nearby, he draped it solicitously over her shoulders.

Gilmary looked up at him with frightened eyes, but said nothing. She was shaking so uncontrollably that her teeth chattered.

For what seemed an eternity, the two of them waited for

Peter and listened intently. Finally, his head appeared above the circular hole. Climbing out, he gently set the lid to the tunnel back in its place.

Leading the way, Emile entered the kitchen first. It was dark, with a pile of soiled plates and coffee cups left in the sink. Someone would have dishes to wash tomorrow, he thought, but not me. Swinging the kitchen door open and craning his neck into the dining room, he checked to see if there were lights on in the living room. Good. All was dark.

Turning back to the other two, Emile said, "The party's over for the bridge group and for us. I bet that theirs was tame compared to ours!"

Meanwhile, Peter had settled Gilmary into a chair that had arms to support her. Crouching before her and taking her hands in his, he gently rubbed them. He figured the warming sensation would calm her.

Gilmary just stared straight ahead and trembled. Finally, her eyes focused on Peter. Slowly a smile spread across her face. "He fell for our ploy—hook, line and sinker. He thinks all of the weapons are in the Casemates, not in the American Cem...." Her voice and smile faded as she realized her slip-up. She hadn't told Peter about her adventure with Tilly and the two young boys, Iggy and Renzo. Peter wouldn't have wanted her or anyone else to know about what was hidden at the cemetery.

Frowning in consternation, Peter stopped rubbing her hands. Softly he said, "Shush, I don't know how you know this, but we won't discuss it in front of Emile. Later!"

Emile, who was busy at the stove boiling water for tea, heard none of their conversation. Now as the kettle began to whistle, he turned gleefully towards the other two. "Hilda," he chortled in a high-pitched falsetto. "Why did you follow me? Why must you always horn in on all of my fun? Don't you have your own fun and games at the mental hospital?" Then he laughed at his own parody.

"You can really think on your feet, cousin. That improvisation was brilliant. Did you see how livid she became? She would have killed you on the spot if Feldmeier didn't have his gun trained on her."

"And me... his gun was also aimed at me!" interjected Gilmary.

Peter rose to his feet and handed her a cup of tea. He was pleased to see her react favorably to Emile's banter. That young man could defuse any tense situation. And yes, her timely improvisation probably saved her life. Of course, he and Emile had helped too.

Emile, with a steaming cup in hand, brought a chair over and joined the other two at the table. "You know, I'm really sorry Beata and I leave later this morning to go back to Paris. That international hive of spies will seem dull after this. All of the action seems to be under the von Hollenden roof."

"You are literally right, Emile. What would mother think if she knew we're living above a powder keg?" asked Gilmary, while looking at Peter. "What if the Soviets decide to destroy all of that stuff by blowing it up and therefore keeping it out of NATO's hands?"

Peter interjected. "That won't happen. You see, even though there appears to be lots of ammo stored there, in reality, all of the cartridges are filled with sand. Not a one could possibly do any damage. It's all a big charade!"

Looking sharply at both of them, he continued. "I didn't think I'd ever have to admit that to you, but there it is! So much planning and now so few secrets. You must never even intimate that the ammo is not live."

"What about Feldmeier?" Gilmary asked skeptically. "Do you think he's already on his way to Berlin?"

Emile leaned forward towards Peter. "Yes, did you see him when you went back into the caverns?"

"No, but I know he left because he closed the heavy door

and locked it. Olga had skedaddled too. I don't blame her. He wanted to kill her—and you," remarked Peter, looking at the nun. "I think he doesn't like women."

Gilmary smiled smugly. "That's because we outsmart him. Seriously though, do you think both of them will have left Luxembourg City by the afternoon? Wouldn't Olga feel that it's too dangerous to stay behind just to kill me? And Herr Feldmeier—he must be galloping east as fast as he can to deliver his news and bask in the glory of his coup."

Peter responded. "If I were Feldmeier, I'd leave immediately. He wants the recognition he'll get for being the first to tell the Soviets where we are storing arms here in Luxembourg. But Olga, for months, has been planning the showdown we witnessed below in the caverns. Now all of her dreams are shattered. That's why she might hang around and try again to get rid of you. She's the imminent danger."

Emile's dark eyes clouded with concern as he looked at his cousin. Would danger ever give up stalking her, he wondered.

Gilmary's natural optimism asserted itself. "I think Olga is relishing my being left behind by Feldmeier to die amidst the crates of weapons, which are supposed to save us from Soviet destruction. After all, I didn't emerge from the caverns, and the East Berliner locked the only exit. I'm doomed in her mind."

Peter, who was still wide awake, feigned a yawn and stretched widely. Looking at the kitchen clock, he said, "Three o'clock already. Soon the chickens will be up. Let's call it a night and go to bed."

Chapter Twenty-Eight

Gilmary had a difficult time falling asleep, but finally it happened. Now, a few hours later, when a sunbeam settled over her eyes, she awoke, finding the house entirely quiet. She wondered what time it was. Then she remembered it was Sunday—the day Emile and Beata were leaving. Jumping out of bed, she made for the bathroom down the hall. There she found the hamper overflowing with damp towels—evidence that everyone else had showered before her.

Twenty minutes later, bounding down the stairs while adjusting her veil over damp, disheveled auburn hair, Gilmary expected to see suitcases stacked by the front hall door. But there were none. Crestfallen, she guessed Emile and Beata had already left, and she had missed saying good-bye to Beata. She'd become fond of Emile's girlfriend. I hope she had a good time here, she thought, even though she'd been roped into an unexpected bridge party.

Now as she turned towards the living room, she heard the rustling of newspaper. Peter, partially obscured by the paper, looked up at her and offered, "Would you like someone to read the comics to you, little girl?"

"No, old man, I can read them myself, thank you. But what's with the little girl stuff? Don't you know you are addressing Mata Hari?"

"Well, you looked so crestfallen, that I thought you needed some cheering up."

Gilmary plopped herself ungracefully onto the sofa next to Peter. "It's Sunday and not only did I miss Mass, but I missed seeing off Emile and Beata. What a bummer!"

Peter smiled at the crestfallen Mata Hari. "There, there. I have an idea."

"You and your ideas are always dangerous—at least for me! Save the idea for another time. I'm going for a walk." Then Gilmary abruptly rose from the sofa and headed for the hall closet to get her trench coat.

"Just a minute, Mata Hari! You're missing your disguise."

"What disguise do I need in my own city? You yourself said Feldmeier has most certainly left for Berlin and Olga's probably also run from here as fast as her wobbly legs can take her. So what's the problem?"

"The problem is that a few hours ago in the kitchen, we were just speculating about your two nemeses leaving already. They may have reasoned differently from us, and so there could still be danger for you," argued Peter, desperately hoping to keep Gilmary from leaving the house.

Returning her trench coat to the closet and coming reluctantly back into the living room Gilmary plopped into a wing chair across from Peter and looked glumly at the CIA agent. "Am I always going to be a prisoner in my own house? Truly, I wouldn't have signed on for this adventure if I had known I'd have to sacrifice my freedom—forever!"

Peter winced at her words. "Don't be so dismal! Disguises are fun. In fact, let me show you how fun it can be."

Gilmary impatiently sat still while Peter combed flour into her hair. "What if it rains? Then the flour will run down my face and glue my eyelids shut," she whined.

"The rain was last night, and now it's as bright a day as

you could ever want. There isn't a hint of rain on the horizon. Just sit still! We have to improvise to make your hair gray, since I don't have enough dye to do both your hair and mine. I wouldn't want to get flour from my hair onto your grandfather's brown homburg."

Gilmary looked out of the corner of her eyes at him. "So instead you want to get flour on my grandmother's hat. What would she think of that?"

"Well, I think she'd approve of our using their old clothes that your mother had saved in the trunk in the cellar. After all, she wouldn't want you to go out as yourself and take a chance of getting shot. Most grandmothers are quite protective of their offspring."

Gilmary grumbled and squirmed as Peter took her face in his hands to critique his handiwork. "The hair is fine. Now we have to make your skin look older. For that, first we'll coat your face in white clay and let it dry. Then we can sponge it off and use make-up to sketch in some creases near your eyes and mouth."

"Who am I supposed to be anyway? And why do I have to look old?"

"You, dear lady, are my old spinster sister, Irmengard Metzler. I'm going to accompany you to Vespers this evening at the Cathedral. You would like that, wouldn't you?"

Gilmary sputtered indignantly. "Your old spinster sister! That's creepy!"

"It may be a little creepy, but it's fun, and a great disguise, I think. With the right posture and leisurely gait, you'll be able to fool even your neighbors. Let's hope they don't recognize your grandparents' clothing, although I doubt if anyone would remember their clothing after so many years."

Peter was having a great time transforming the young nun into an old lady. It was even more fun because she was balking at the process. Nevertheless, it took her mind off of her forced confinement and gave her imagination a chance to create a new persona.

Finally content with his handiwork, he sent Gilmary off to her room to put on her grandmother's clothes. When she returned, she appeared to be a discouraged old woman.

"Liven up, sister!" demanded Peter. "You are getting out on the town soon, even if it's only to Vespers. Afterwards, when dusk has fallen, we can take a stroll along the esplanade. You can contemplate all that had happened since your stroll last evening with the Soviet agent."

Then putting all of his disguise tools away in their box, he turned to look at her once more. "While I'm dressing as Dr. Sigmund Metzler, you can practice having a stooped posture and walking slowly, almost labored, with a slight limp. You can get the limp by not bending one knee as you walk. Try it in front of the hall mirror. It'll be good practice for your old age," he teased her good-naturedly.

"That's not even funny! You are a most callous doctor. Even an academic doctor ought to have more feeling and empathy."

Chapter Twenty-Nine

Hurriedly shutting the door behind her, Olga strode down the dark lane between ancient houses that leaned towards each other in this forgotten corner of Luxembourg City. Her hiking boots made a scrapping noise on the damp, uneven cobblestones. At this early hour, it was the only noise echoing off the old walls, if you didn't count the gurgling and dripping raindrops coursing down the gutters.

She'd chosen to rent a room in this part of the old city because it was hidden away in the groin of the deep chasm of the Alzette River. Although from its streets it had a view of the Bock Casemates above it, no tourists came here since there were other more favorable spots to view the famous fortifications.

The added advantage to this neighborhood was its proximity to the train station in which direction she was headed now. Having checked the schedule and finding the next train was leaving for Cologne at seven o'clock that morning, she packed quickly. She needed a ticket out of town. It would be all the better, too, if Herr Feldmeier would be a fellow passenger. She fervently hoped he would be because eventually she had a score to settle with him.

Fearing he'd try to kill her again if he recognized her on the journey they would each be taking to East Berlin, she had taken meticulous care in applying her disguise. She'd outfitted herself before as a young man—an adventurous university student on holiday, intent on doing some hiking in the Elbe Sandstone

Mountains of East Germany. No one had ever given the slightest indication that they thought her otherwise.

Now, as the early morning breeze was scuttling the evening's rain clouds towards the east, she climbed the hill out of the gloomy chasm from which fog was billowing in gentle waves. Shifting her backpack and using the mountain-climbing pole for balance, she acknowledged that the night's exertions and lack of sleep were draining her energy. The shot of adrenaline from her encounter with Feldmeier and her doppelganger had dissipated entirely. In its place, a bone-numbing weariness had settled in. What she had thought would be the triumphal climax to her scheme, now seemed to only be a blip on the roadmap. Certainly, getting herself reinstated into the confidence of the Stasi hierarchy was proving difficult.

If she could arrive in Berlin before Feldmeier, however, and present the coveted information about the Luxembourgish "stay-behind" army's hidden cache of weapons, then the Stasi and Soviets would have reason to trust her again.

Comrade Feldmeier, she determined, was no match for her as far as skill. If she'd known of his intent to kill her and the nun, she'd have been ready for him. Then he'd be the corpse secreted in the locked cavern. The thought of the cavern filled with crates gave her a mental picture of her double, the unfortunate nun, dying in despair—not a pleasant thought really. Since the nun was the very image of herself, Olga felt queasy, as if a part of her was dying too.

What if they really were twins? No, it wasn't possible. Her mother would have told her, or someone would have whispered it to her at some time over the years, even if only as a playground taunt.

There were only a couple of dozen people mulling around the platform as they waited to board the early outgoing train to Cologne. The later ten o'clock train would be more popular. Either way, the passengers from Luxembourg had to disembark at

Cologne if they were continuing on their journey and proceed to other trains. There was no direct train from Luxembourg to Berlin.

Olga unobtrusively scanned the clique of travelers, but saw no one who could be Feldmeier, even in disguise. Somehow, though, she didn't think he would consider a disguise for himself. He'd be too confident that he had gotten rid of those meddling women.

From inside the 2nd class car that advertised it was destined for Cologne, Comrade Feldmeier gazed at the platform through the crack between the half-drawn curtain and the window. There were the usual families with children returning home early after a short weekend in Luxembourg. Then there were the youth hostel crowd, always looking a little scruffy.

Earlier, he'd managed to unobtrusively slide past the guard, who was keeping passengers from boarding before the train was ready for them. Being the first on board had the advantage of his choosing an empty compartment for himself, drawing the curtains and locking the door. It gave him peace of mind not having to worry about being recognized. Maybe he could even catch some sleep. He certainly could use some, since he wanted to be alert so he could savor every moment of his meeting with his superiors in Berlin. Sinking into his seat, he closed his eyes in his first chance at relaxation in twenty-four hours.

"Achtung! Was ist losee? Why is this door locked?"

Feldmeier was shocked awake by the racket at the door. Rubbing his eyes, he glanced at the doorknob which was frenetically snapping back and forth.

"Einen Moment bitte," he shouted as he reached forward to unlock the compartment door.

"I'm sorry," he said to the conductor. "I just needed some uninterrupted sleep." Then he handed the man his passport and ticket.

The conductor's large shoulders blocked the small doorway, but as he reached for the man's identity papers, Feldmeier looked past him and into the aisle beyond. Just then, passing the compartment was a young, blond man with a cap pulled low over his forehead. For a moment their eyes met. The East Berliner thought that he saw a shock of recognition in the young man's clear eyes.

Were the eyes blue? Certainly not dark. Maybe green. But why would he recognize me? Is he one of the Poles who ate in the back room at Chez Maurice? Puzzled, he returned his papers to his inner pocket and sat down.

Back in her compartment, Olga shivered. The woman sitting opposite her looked up and wondered if the young blond man had a chill. Certainly he looked slender and a little delicate—not manly like the men in her family.

Turning her head away from her compartment mates, Olga gazed unseeingly out of the window. Glimpsing Herr Feldmeier in the compartment next to her left her shaken. It was too soon to have to deal with him; she hadn't formulated a plan for annihilating him. But as fate would have it, here they were, locked in a race to get to Berlin—and on the same train.

Finally focusing on the cars whizzing past the tracks, she realized the autobahn followed the same route as the train, only the cars were going much faster. Both routes curved parallel to each other towards a small hamlet one could barely see more than a mile ahead.

Aloud she said, "That's it!" Three heads looked up as she sprang to her feet, grabbed her knapsack and pole and hurried out of the compartment.

Bumping along the narrow passage, she continued away from the compartment where she had glimpsed Feldmeier. Once in the next tight passage where two of the rail cars met and shifted with the movement of the wheels, she pulled the emergency brake. Immediately, there followed a terrible screech

175

as the speeding cars tried to slow.

Olga knew it would take a quarter of a mile to finally stop, and that they had already passed the hamlet a half mile ago.

Nevertheless, she had confidence that she could hitch a ride on the autobahn. With luck she could be in Cologne an hour before the Soviet agent and on to Berlin before him too.

Comrade Feldmeier was shaken awake again. The train was slowing with urgency, and there was a terrible noise—a high-pitched, irritating screech. Now what was happening, he wondered. Panicking for a moment, he tore the curtains aside. While he watched the neat farm fields slide by, he suddenly saw a knapsack and pole fly through the air and land in the gully between the autobahn and the tracks. Astonished, he next saw a body fly out from the train, curl itself into a ball and roll down the grassy embankment towards the highway.

Someone, he calculated, had to get off this train urgently. Why? With a groan, the image of Olga Diederich formed in his mind. It couldn't be, could it?

Chapter Thirty

The incense, flickering candle light, and chanting voices—these were a balm that calmed Gilmary's soul. Gradually she relaxed. Even Peter, kneeling next to her, appeared to be more at peace than he had been in weeks.

Looking down at her grandmother's dress, which hung loosely around her frame, the nun imagined herself as her grandmother. She did feel older. Could it be that a disguise could influence your mind that much?

Glancing at Peter, she smiled. He certainly looked like someone who could be a professor of post-medieval architecture. Sigmund Metzler was a very distinguished-sounding name. But Irmengard! What a yucky name, that one.

When the congregation filed out of the cathedral, they had to adjust their eyes from the light inside the cathedral to the gloom of dusk. With Gilmary leaning on Peter's arm for support, the elderly-appearing couple strolled towards the esplanade.

Interspersed between the lamps set around the crescent promenade, were lovely, wrought-iron benches of a unique style. They were fashioned in a serpentine design formed like an "S" so that one occupant looked one way and the other person faced the other direction.

Gilmary stiffly lowered herself onto one seat while Peter took the other. "Aren't these the best benches for viewing the Petrusse Valley?" asked Gilmary. "You can keep your eyes peeled that way for invading Huns, and I can keep the western exposure under control."

Peter chuckled, "And from which direction do you expect Herr Feldmeier to advance?"

"Personally, I'm sure we would only see the back of him receding. He has to be on his way to Berlin. Being as paranoid as all of these agents are, he wouldn't trust anyone else to relay the valuable information back to the mucky-mucks at headquarters."

Peter nodded. "You're right. That's one thing all spies have in common. They don't trust other spies—even those working in the same network. Each one wants to take full credit for an intelligence scoop."

Gilmary slouched in her seat and lifted her head to look at the moon. "You know, I don't feel frightened anymore. It's as if there's no danger. I'm protected."

"I'm glad you feel so secure," replied Peter.

"Well, think of it," continued the nun. "Here we are spinning around the universe on earth and we could fly off any second, but gravity holds us here securely. We don't have to want it or will it or even be aware of it. It just holds us here as if we were in the hand of God."

Peter observed, "You are in a philosophical mood tonight."

"I feel now as if I wasn't really in any danger last night. The Holy Spirit was prompting me to confuse Herr Feldmeier by calling Olga Hilda, my twin."

"I thought the Holy Spirit would only inspire you to say the truth," rejoined Peter.

"How do we know that it isn't the truth? Maybe she is my twin."

"I think your mother would beg to differ. She'd consider Olga the spawn of the devil. No, you can't hang Olga on your parents!"

Gilmary drew a deep breath. "One has to feel sorry for

her, though. She's on such a strange and futile quest. Don't you think that being a child in Germany during the war made it almost impossible for her to have a trusting relationship with the world?"

Peter drew out his pipe and lit it as he considered what war could do to a small child. "Yes, it's probably impossible to regain trust if you don't have the shelter of a family that gives you the confidence that you're part of a nurturing community. We don't know what forces influenced Olga after the war, but we can see their after-affects and how they stunted her social development."

Changing the subject, Gilmary turned to face Peter. "What will you do now, Sigmund? By the way, I like that name for you. I think that going forward, I'll always think of you as my accomplished brother, Siggy. No, I guess Siggy is too pedestrian of a moniker. You are truly a Sigmund."

Bowing his head slightly, Peter grinned. "That's very fine of you, Irmengard."

"Irmengard! Why do I have to be the Irmengard to your Sigmund?"

"Don't you like your name? It's a very singular one—no one else has it as far as I know, and you like to be distinctive."

"It's nice to not be lost in a crowd of Debbies or Judys, but Sister Gilmary of St. Dominic is distinctive enough for me."

"Well then, I'll think of you as my sister Gilmary, or Philomena."

Gilmary felt satisfied now that she wouldn't be a permanent Irmengard. "Getting back to my question. What will you do now? Or better said what will that puppet master, Arthur Leventhal, have you doing next?"

"Arthur at this moment is probably designing some complicated trap for me to spring or to have sprung on me. Maybe he'll send me back to Salzburg so I can be found again by the lovely Austrian go-between."

Gilmary raised her eyebrows expressively. "Is the name

of that little lovely also Odette Millon?"

"As a matter of fact, no. It's Renata Friedhof."

"That's a curious name. Renata comes from the Latin and means 'reborn', while Friedhof in German can mean 'cemetery'. Not many folks get reborn in a cemetery."

"Humm, you're right. It is curious."

"Well, if I were you, I'd keep my distance from anyone claiming to be reborn in a cemetery full of old bones."

"Come on Irmengard," urged Peter taking her arm to help her stand. "It's time for all of us old folks to go home, watch the news on the telly, and go to bed."

Chapter Thirty-One

The day was gray and damp with a constant drizzle. Locals called it "Dutch weather" because it was the typical spring weather of the lowlands near the Atlantic. Today however, the wind had blown the dampness inland and cast its net over the valleys of Luxembourg.

When Gretta Kolnberger entered the Freistadt Bank, she brought the weather in with her. Energetically flapping the ribs of her black umbrella, she sprayed droplets all around her. She didn't care. Dieter had seemed rude and distant towards her the last time she'd come here, so she would repay him with a wet lobby.

Behind the grill of his teller's cage, Dieter was going about his business in a black mood. The flow of recent events had turned against him. First, Madame von Hollenden (he wouldn't deign now to call her Genevieve) had shown no warmth as she said good-bye after the bridge party. In his estimation she was now second class. He came to that conclusion because she actually enjoyed learning to play sheepshead—that proletariat card game, so inferior to bridge. Then she'd failed to show some delicate deference towards him, who was a most eligible bachelor. Well, he would shake the dust of her street off of his shoes!

Secondly, Herr Feldmeier had disappeared just when Dieter felt that he was about to enter the inner circle of the Soviet machine here in Luxembourg. Even Hermann Richter didn't seem to know where the East Berliner had gone. Dieter knew the butcher was quite transparent, so he trusted him when he told him that he had no knowledge of the Soviet agent's whereabouts.

Third and finally, "The Marleena D.", his prize rose, was showing signs of the botrytis blight. He had banked on showing his little beauty at the Royal Rose Exposition in June. Now even that pleasure might be denied him.

Forcibly jolted out of his dark mood by the clatter of sharp heels against the wet terrazzo floor, Dieter saw Frau Kolnberger marching towards his teller's cage. Seeing how furiously she looked at him, he politely asked what he could do for her today.

Plunking down her eight francs, she met his eyes in a steady frown, while trying to gauge his mood.

Dieter, who had concluded that the fates were chastising him for some unknown reason, decided he'd better mend his relationship with this comrade. Drawing his finger across his upper lip, he signaled that they should meet at lunchtime at Trois Cygnets.

Seeing his use of their private code, Gretta brightened. He'd have news for her. She would look forward to that since life seemed particularly dull at the moment.

Seated at their favorite table, Dieter and Gretta immediately fell into their usual comfortable, conspiracy mode.

"What's happened to the 'Star of the East' rose?" asked Gretta.

"I'm not sure, but it would seem that its blossom will disappoint us. The last I heard, it was entwined around the Spanish Turret. It has a closed, secretive bud, and may never show itself to full effect."

Gretta's face fell as her bright expression faded. She had such high hopes for the East Berlin agent, whom she had heard about but never met.

Her Italian boarders had discussed among themselves their concerns about him while dining at her table. She could sense he made them nervous. Maybe that was why he'd disappeared—he'd failed to persuade them to join the Communist Party. Too bad! If the Party had a larger, more active membership here in Luxembourg City, she could take her rightful place as a senior leader—one who had worked in the trenches in the early days of the Party. Now, gazing over at the insignificant-looking bank teller she felt old and used up. History had passed them by.

Chapter Thirty-Two

"Where's the milk?" asked Gilmary, as she turned from the refrigerator.

"There isn't any," explained Maria Goretti, "although I know there was some yesterday."

"Darn", growled Gilmary guiltily, as she remembered using the last of it the night before to wash away the traces of clay and make-up from her face. "I'd wanted to make scrambled eggs."

"Just substitute yogurt," offered Maria Goretti. "I've done that when I had no milk."

"Ugh! I remember your yogurt-scrambled eggs. No thanks," Gilmary said with a wry expression on her face.

Making a noisy entrance, Peter came through the kitchen door. "What's this? I didn't expect to find you two up so early this morning."

Looking up at him brightly, the two young nuns made room for him at the table. Putting down her spoon, Maria Goretti said, "Do you think we'd want to be late for work? Our clients may be at the door already, jostling to see who'll be first in line to see us this morning."

"I don't think so," said Peter, frowning. "I'm afraid you're finished being scribes for now."

Maria Goretti looked astonished. "Why? What happened?"

"You two did a fabulous job of making contacts. It's

paid off, and now that the operation's finished, we can close it down."

"Close it down? So suddenly? What will our friends and clients think?" Maria Goretti was incredulous.

Gilmary realized now that Peter was right. There was no need any more for them to keep up their contacts in the migrant community, but the suddenness of their quitting was a jolt to her too. It seemed disloyal to leave the men, who depended on their services, without a replacement.

Peter looked at his two friends. "I'm sorry. It's sudden I know. But that's the nature of this kind of operation. We set it up in order to get information; then we shut it down when we have what we need."

Maria Goretti was feeling deflated and disappointed in Peter. In fact, she felt used. Of course, she knew going into the operation what its purpose was, but now the charade seemed so false.

"What will happen to my Polish workers' social group? They'll think I copped out. My ministry will look self-serving, and I don't want that!"

Peter now understood how attached Maria Goretti felt to her ministry. At the same time he knew it was necessary for the two women to leave Luxembourg. If they stayed, they'd be in danger since Gilmary's cover was now suspect. Eventually, Feldmeier, who probably thought he had gotten rid of the nun-agent in the caverns, might reconsider. If he came back to Luxembourg and found out she was still here, he'd certainly eliminate her. He'd be as afraid of her as she would be of him.

Now looking at their crestfallen faces, Peter made a decision. "Today you can go to the office, Maria Goretti, and have lunch with your sheepshead club. That way, you'll have a chance to say good-bye to them and pass the baton to someone else. Certainly, they can choose a leader and maybe even a sergeant-at-arms to keep order at their meetings. If you're really persuasive, get them to elect a chaplain. Then you can be sure the group continues the way you've planned it."

Maria Goretti smiled tentatively. It was not a perfect solution, but as least she could conclude her work in a worthy manner.

As she rose from the table to go, Peter put his hand on her arm. "After lunch, I'll come around and help you pack up your office supplies and also Gilmary's. I think that together we'll be able to haul it all home in a taxi."

After Maria Goretti left, Peter turned to Gilmary. "Irmengard, you look sad. Do you want to put on all of that make-up and accompany your younger brother to the office after lunch?"

Gilmary shuddered at the thought of putting flour or talcum powder in her hair and clay on her face again. "No Sigmund dear. But could you pick up some milk on your way home? Since I can't leave the house, you get to be errand boy too."

At two o'clock in the afternoon, Maria Goretti returned dejectedly to her office in the foyer of Weicker and Franck. Lunch and the sheepshead game that followed had been fun. The men were emotional, however, when they heard it would be their last meeting with her. Still, they had made good choices in electing their leaders. Nevertheless, she felt like St. Paul leaving his flock in Ephesus to the care of Timothy. Paul had some misgivings too. But Maria Goretti consoled herself with the thought that someday she'd return to Luxembourg and visit her new friends.

Opening the door to her glass cubicle, she was astonished to see an older man balancing a brown hat on his knees as he sat in her chair. Was he to be her last client? Then she chuckled as she recognized Peter in his Sigmund costume. Next to him in the corner, he had piled several large boxes and bags.

"Good afternoon, Doctor Metzler. What a pleasant surprise! It's good of you to come to help me move. I don't know how I could do it without you."

"And how was your leave-taking of the Poles?"

"Just fine," said Maria Goretti softly as she turned away from Peter with tears in her eyes.

Genevieve heard the mail fall through the chute next to the front door. She was hoping to receive news concerning the Royal Rose Exposition set for late June. The last time she had conferred with Arthur, she made sure he realized that she would be fully occupied here in Luxembourg City with the rose exhibition. There would be no espionage for her that month.

Now, as she sorted the mail, she stopped to read the return address of a letter addressed to her daughter. There was one for Maria Goretti also. Both were postmarked Racine, Wisconsin, so they were from St. Catherine's.

Genevieve sighed as she put the two letters on the table. No doubt someone at the convent was giving them new orders. She knew she only had the two of them on loan, but dreaded their leaving.

Nathan was gone to American; now they would be leaving too. She would be left with only her friends and her roses. Would they be enough for her? As she became older, it was harder to make the adjustment to being alone.

Well, maybe dear Arthur would conjure up some exploit for her after the rose season. The thought of Arthur and his surprises lightened her mood as she went to give the letter to her daughter.

Gilmary frowned at first as she examined the return address. She'd been so busy fighting the Cold War that she'd forgotten about her life in Racine.

Tearing open the envelope, she extracted a small piece of paper folded over just once. It was a familiar size and shape, and yes, today was near to the end of May, time for assignments. It read:

Sisters of Saint Dominic
Convent of St. Catherine
Racine, Wisconsin.
Office of the Mother General
Assignment in Holy Obedience.

Venerable Sister Gilmary,
you have been assigned to the mission of
St. Catherine High School
for the year 1965 - 1966
Dated May 18th
Mother Assumpta, O.P.
Mother General

Thoughtfully, she fingered the small piece of paper. St. Catherine's High School. Most likely she'd resume teaching German and Russian. Nostalgically, she pictured some of her students. Of course, it was easiest to picture the trouble-makers, but even those she remembered fondly. Secretly, even though she would have to leave her mother and home again, she was happy to know what she'd be doing for the next year. Also, there was little danger from Soviet agents in a small city in Wisconsin. Yes, she could use the tranquility of teaching again and being a part of the religious community.

"What are we going to do with all of these dictionaries? Should we store them or give them away?" Maria Goretti was stacking the books she and Peter had retrieved from their cubicles at Weicker and Franck on the desk in the von Hollenden library.

Peter had helped her cart the boxes into the house and then left to do errands, still disguised as Professor Metzler.

Genevieve glanced wistfully at the young nun. "My dear, don't you worry about the dictionaries. I'll just shelf them here for the next time you and Gilmary need to act as scribes." In truth, she was dreading their leaving. She expected they would need to be gone within a day or two. How empty and quiet the house would be then.

With a heavy sigh, Maria Goretti placed the two typewriters on a shelf and covered them. "I can't even guess where and when that'll be. But it was fun, and we made a lot of friends through our work. Even my Polish improved—but I don't know when it'll ever come in handy again."

With a quick step, Gilmary entered the library waving an envelope in the air. "Open it, open it! Let's see if it's the same as my letter from Racine."

Grabbing the envelope, Maria Goretti carefully slit it open and slid out a small piece of paper. Reading it thoughtfully, she didn't react for a moment. She was still feeling her disappointment at leaving the Polish and Italian workers and closing up shop as a scribe. Finally, a tear appeared and started its journey down her cheek and to the corner of her mouth. Another one followed. Turning to Genevieve, she embraced her.

"You've been so wonderful—just like my own mother—but more than that. You've been my friend too. And you even started to learn sheepshead! What more could a friend ask of another? I'm going to miss you so much."

Now Genevieve was overcome with empathy. Grabbing her handkerchief, she gently dabbed at Maria Goretti's tear-stained cheek, then kissed her on each cheek and gave her a hug. With her feelings too strong to speak, she quickly left the room.

Gilmary took the rest of the supplies from their scribe's office and organized them in the drawers of the library desk while she waited for her friend to compose herself. Finally, Maria

Goretti sat down and said in a dull voice, "I'm assigned to teach third grade at St. Ignatius School."

"Don't make it sound like a death sentence. Third grade is the best! You know you love kids that age. They're still innocent and excited about learning just about anything you put before them. You can start by teaching them some Polish greetings. That ought to get them interested! Then you can do a project where you cut out those lovely paper roosters and stuff. I'll even help you get the supplies together."

While Gilmary talked, Maria Goretti folded the letter from Racine into an origami bird. When she was satisfied that it looked like it would fly, she sent it sailing across the room and laughed. "You're right, of course. Third grade is the best. I'm actually lucky they gave me eight-year-olds to teach. They're so enthusiastic. It will probably be like having a roomful of Iggys and Renzos. I wonder who else will be living at the convent at St. Ignatius. There'd better be a really good cook. Otherwise, I'll be over to your place for a few meals."

"You ought to have Mother Assumpta put an asterisk next to your name, with a note to always assign you to a convent with great food. Like the army, you travel on your stomach."

Maria Goretti chuckled at the thought of Mother Assumpta considering as a top priority the cook who is assigned to a convent house. Not a bad idea, though. If Saint Teresa of Avila thought that cleanliness was next to godliness, then the Maria Goretti rule would be that good food makes a happy community. In fact, if she ever were to become the mother general, she would hire Emile and Beata to start a cooking school at the motherhouse so that their order of nuns would be known for the best cooks. Young women would be queued outside the doors clamoring to join their community.

Snapping out of her delightful daydream, Maria Goretti rose from her chair and moved towards the door. "I'd better begin to pack. It seems like events are moving fast now."

At five o'clock, as the shadows were lengthening, the doorbell rang. Upon opening the door, Genevieve found a delivery man on the porch. "I have a package for Madame von Hollenden," the young man said deferentially, as he handed her a long, white box.

Thanking him, she closed the door and set the box on the table, then opened it uncertainly. She hadn't been expecting any delivery, and the box had no return address. As the lid came off, she gasped in surprise and admiration. Nestled in a bed of green floral paper were a dozen deep pink roses. While reading the message that came with the blooms, a smile spread over her face. The flowers were from Arthur Leventhal. How thoughtful and timely. He probably knew she'd feel forgotten once her daughter and Maria Goretti left for the States.

"Who was at the door? Oh my, what lovely roses! Who are they from?" Gilmary's curiosity piqued as she entered the room and saw her mother's flushed face.

Fast on her tail followed Peter, who had come home an hour ago. Looking at the blush of happiness suffusing Genevieve's face, he felt that someone whom she admired had sent the flowers.

Waving the card at them, she exclaimed, "These roses are from Arthur, and there are twelve of them. In case, you don't know the language of flowers, twelve deep pink roses mean he is expressing his gratitude." Glancing up at her daughter, she explained, "When your father was alive, he often sent me a dozen red roses. That was symbolic of his undying love for me, or, as he said, his passion for me. He was an old-fashioned romantic."

Gilmary put her arm around her mother's waist and gave her a kiss on the cheek. "You know, Arthur is full of surprises. Maybe someday he'll send you a dozen red roses too."

Genevieve laughed merrily. "Arthur is too busy sending

his minions out to chase spies to think of romance. But he is very charming."

Turning next to Maria Goretti, Peter produced another small box. Maria Goretti let out a gasp. She certainly hadn't expected to be specially remembered by Peter. A minute later, she laughed ecstatically as he tied a red ribbon around her neck. Hanging on the ribbon was a round medallion with the Polish eagle etched upon it.

That evening after dinner, Peter explained how tomorrow the two young nuns would leave Luxembourg on a late afternoon flight to the States. Because he wanted to be absolutely sure no harm would come to them on their journey, he wanted them to dress in regular clothes instead of their blue suits and veils. That way, if anyone was on the lookout for them, they wouldn't be recognizable. Then he gave Genevieve a small package. She looked up at him questioningly before beginning to unwrap the present. Inside was an elegantly wrought, silver rosebud pin. Rising to her feet and with tears in her eyes, she embraced the young man who had helped her so much and in so many ways.

Turning next to Maria Goretti, Peter produced another small box. Maria Goretti let out a gasp. She certainly hadn't expected to be specially remembered by Peter. A minute later, she laughed ecstatically as he tied a red ribbon around her neck. Hanging on the ribbon was a round medallion with the Polish eagle etched upon it.

"I had Krzysztof draw the Polish emblem for me, and then I took it to a jeweler to etch it on this medallion. This way you have a token to help you remember your adventure here in Luxembourg."

"Oh, Peter! How thoughtful you are. I'll always treasure this. Of course, we do have a vow of poverty, so we own nothing ourselves. I may have to let the other nuns wear it sometimes. Who knows, it may become an honored emblem for our whole community!"

Then Peter paused behind Gilmary's chair. With a small, courtly bow he said, "I have a gift for you also, Irmengard. But you'll have to come out on the terrace to receive it."

"Is it that big? Could it be a howitzer?"

"Just you wait and see!"

Later that evening, Peter presented his gift to her as they sat together on the terrace. Since it was a rather small box, Gilmary decided that it couldn't be a howitzer—not that she wanted one. Instead, she found a miniature model of the S-shaped chairs like those that graced the crescent on the esplanade. Looking over at Peter, she expressed her gratitude. "That was a special night. We both felt so much relief since our plan to confuse Herr Feldmeier had worked."

"Yes, we were relieved. But it was your philosophizing that impressed me that evening. And, of course, there was the fun of seeing you disguised as my elderly, spinster sister."

"Don't tell Nathan, or he'll always refer to me as his spinster sister."

Reaching into his pocket, Peter retrieved his pipe and proceeded to fill it. While he drew on the stem until he was satisfied, Gilmary gazed at the night sky, which was reflecting back the glow of city lights. Calmness had descended on them and on the city.

Turning to the nun seated beside him, Peter broke the comfortable silence. "Now you must tell me about how you knew that there are secrets buried in the American Cemetery along with the bodies of some of the most valiant soldiers the world has ever seen."

As Gilmary recounted the story of how she and Tilly had rescued the two young Italian boys from the excavation site in the cemetery, her eyes danced with the recollected excitement of that day. "The really dicey part was when Hermann Richter showed up in a car with Feldmeier. I was still inside the walls and only knew from Tilly that we finally had help. You can imagine my horror when the bucket brought me over the wall, and I saw who our helpers were. When they saw me, they were equally astounded. It was a close call, and to this day, I don't know what they made of it."

"I would wager the East Berliner began to have doubts about you then. But that's old business, since he now figures you're dead. How about Tilly and the boys? Do you think either of the boys noticed the crates in the hole? And would they have said anything about them to Tilly?"

"The hole was full of very wet mud, and I only discovered the boxes when I hit my shins on them. Probably Iggy didn't see the ends of the crates. The thought of being buried alive had so frightened him that what was in the mud, no doubt, didn't register."

"Good. Nevertheless, our men must secure the work site better. If two little boys can figure out how to sneak into the cemetery, it's a sure bet any suspicious agent could do it even easier. Our best defense is their believing all of the weapons are in the Casemates."

Gilmary turned to face Peter directly. Looking at him with sympathy, she said, "Your work is never done, is it?"

"No, Irmengard." Then taking the small model of the S-shaped chair from her hand and gently tapping each small seat with the stem of his pipe, he continued philosophically, "If you will keep the west in view, I'll keep the east in my sights. Together we'll mount a concerted defense for freedom!"

Chapter Thirty-Three

Cautiously leaning against a soot-stained pilaster of a nondescript building facing Friedrichstrasse, Olga felt the tender bruise on her left shoulder-blade. She had hit the ground hard as she hurled herself from the train onto the embankment; now she was paying for her spontaneous decision. Nevertheless, here she was only yards away from East Berlin, which she could glimpse through the constant rain that acted like a thin, tired curtain masking the dismal stage-set before her.

As lightning streaked across the eastern sky, she counted the seconds to gauge where it had struck. The Stasi headquarters were only three miles away, but the rumbling thunder took six counts to reveal itself. She had been contemplating how she would make her entrance into that formidable bastion of state security ever since she managed to thumb a ride from some naïve students on holiday. Her decision to dump the train in favor of catching a ride on the Autobahn had certainly put her ahead of Herr Feldmeier, who could just now be crossing the border from West Germany into the Soviet Eastern sector. But he had his identity papers; she did not. That small detail was what now stalled her final sprint into East Berlin.

Hoisting her backpack onto her right shoulder-blade, she hunched her back and dashed into the rain towards Checkpoint Charlie. As her hiking boots splashed the water from the uneven pavement up onto her pants legs, she could feel the drops, like cold fingers, dribbling down the inside of her socks. Cars were queuing up as they stopped to show their credentials to the American soldiers on this side and then the East German soldiers on the Soviet side. Skirting the fender of an Audi, she saw the sign for the Adler Café. Nostalgically, she remembered its inner golden glow from her days of training three years ago here in Berlin. At that time, her group of recruits had to practice exiting and reentering East Berlin through Checkpoint Charlie. Often in the warmth of the café, they would cool their heels and perhaps don an alternate disguise in order to trick the Americans, who examined their papers critically. She could still envision the café's lavatory with its cracked mirror and dim light, as she had applied makeup and tucked her hair into a silly wig.

At the door, Olga brushed shoulders with a young British soldier, who was entering at the same time. With irritation, she considered how rude he was not to hold the door for her. The Italian men were much more gallant. Then she remembered she was disguised as a young man, so, of course, he would think it was every man for himself. Nevertheless, she growled, *"Dummkopf"* at him. He growled back, *"Du bis."*

Moving into the steamy interior, Olga decided that what she remembered as the café's golden glow was on this rainy day more like the distasteful yellowing of an old smoker's teeth.

Grabbing a chair at a small table in the rear near the hallway to the lavatories, she ordered a lager and leaned back to contemplate how, without the requisite papers, she would trick the authorities into letting her cross the checkpoint. Her idle gaze was arrested by the young soldier she had encountered upon entering. He sat at the table next to hers, but closer to the windows. In the dim light, she thought she could make out the word "interpreter" on the tag prominently displayed on his chest. Watching him carefully, she observed his right hand reach into the inner pocket of his jacket and extract a cigarette case and a lighter. He also must have his identity papers filed there, she speculated.

After a couple of minutes, Olga picked up her stein of beer and nonchalantly made her way towards the man. With what she thought was a manly, slightly rakish smile; she took a chair opposite the youngster and spoke in German.

"*Prost!* It's a day for ducks, I say."

As the boy looked up in surprise which immediately turned to chagrin when he recognized the rude fellow he had bumped into at the door, Olga touched her glass to his in a toast of camaraderie. He nodded his head disinterestedly.

"Would you mind if I bummed a fag off you? I'm afraid mine got all soggy from standing out in the rain. I'll have to part with a few fennings to get a cigarette case like yours if I'm to deal with weather like this."

Reaching across the table, the interpreter offered his case and then reluctantly lit Olga's cigarette. Leaning back in his seat, he pocketed his case and the lighter and patted his chest reassuringly. Olga's eyes took in everything while trying to look disinterested.

"I see you're an interpreter. Are you waiting for some bigwigs, who only speak one language—and that badly—to cross the border?"

Eyeing his unexpected companion through the hazy smoke he exhaled from his nostrils, the interpreter snorted. "You misspeak. They're usually not bigwigs, but old men going bald. But yes, I'm waiting for a carload of them. They need a Russian interpreter, and it's my turn on the rotation." Abruptly, he rose, snubbed out his cigarette and excused himself to the lavatory.

Making a snap decision, Olga's chair legs squealed as she rose quickly and turned to follow the young man into the lavatory. He had stopped to examine his oiled pompadour in the dirty mirror. Approaching him as he bent towards his image, Olga grabbed his shoulders, and spun him around to face her. Then she whipped off her cap and let her blonde hair cascade down her back. His immediate reaction was a loud gasp.

"You're... you're a woman!"

Before he could crank out any more evident observations, Olga rose onto the tips of her toes, grabbed him in a firm clutch and planted a sultry kiss on his lips. This left him stunned and speechless. Then the Stasi agent spun around and marched out of the lavatory.

Smiling to herself, Olga pulled her hair into a bun and stashed it back into the damp cap. Quickly she slid the young man's identity papers into her inner pocket and attached his interpreter badge to her outer pocket. All was well!

The rain had intensified, if that was possible, while she had been in the Adler Café. Now, as she raced out into the deluge, she slid crazily towards a black sedan with tinted windows. Opening the back door, she threw her backpack on the floor and wedged her body into the small space left in the back seat.

"Greetings, I'm your Russian interpreter!" Then taking out the purloined identity papers, she perused them for her new name. It was Adolph Leach. What a strange, hybrid name, being so German and so British. He was proficient in Russian, German and English. Well, she certainly was conversant in Russian and German, but English? When she had a chance, she would change that to Italian. Right now, she hoped that no one would speak to her in English. Her knowledge of that language was mostly confined to swear words.

Hastily, she shuffled the papers back into her pocket and settled back into the seat. Everyone's eyes, except the driver's, were trained on her. Staring back at them confidently, she asked them in German if they were pleased with the weather. After they had all laughed politely, the tension dissipated, and the man in the front seat turned around. Meanwhile, the two balding men in the back seat moved further away from the wet clothes of their new interpreter.

Aware that her wetness was creating a damp atmosphere

in the previously comfortable car, Olga tried to calculate how long before she could surprise them all by jumping out as precipitously as she had entered. First, however, they would have to present their papers, and there were three cars already ahead of them in the pipeline. Impatiently, she pictured Oskar Feldmeier climbing the steps two at a time in the echoing staircases of the Stasi headquarters. No, he wouldn't get there before her! Of that she felt certain.

Standing across the street from the Stasi headquarters, officially known as the Ministry for State Security, Olga looked up at the modernistic building that housed hundreds of employees, minions tasked with gauging the rhythm of the pulse of comrades everywhere. No, actually, they tried to set the rhythm—a formidable job which needed the eyes and ears of a million professional and voluntary spies around the world. How could one building suck in so much information?

Knowing the entrance to the behemoth was around the block, she skirted two corners and came finally to the expansive courtyard. As she approached the guards at the entrance, a medium-sized man in a black overcoat and fedora was just disappearing through the inner door. Ah, the ubiquitous black overcoat! As Olga's heart began to race in fear that she had not beaten Feldmeier after all, she reasoned with herself that black was a color all spies cloaked themselves in at some time or other.

After she had run the gauntlet of security including the thorough inspection of herself and her backpack, Olga entered the monotonous corridor with doors at predictably equal intervals and found a bank of elevators. She was relieved; no one in a black overcoat was to be found anywhere on this floor. Gazing up at the dials above each elevator, she found one of them had stopped at the fifth floor—the same floor she'd been directed to. It was where the Department of Foreign Armament Information was to be found. This made her jittery. Nervously tapping the up button three times, she started to chew her lip as she waited for the dial arrow to subtract numbers back down to one.

Once inside, as the elevator car slowly ascended to the fifth floor, Olga closed her eyes and debated whether she ought to take her cap off and let her hair tumble down so she would be recognizable as a woman, or whether she should stay in disguise just in case the door opened on the fifth floor and she ended up staring into the formidable visage of Herr Feldmeier. When the door finally did slide open, she took a deep breath and opened her eyes. What met her gaze was a frosted-glass door advertising the Department of Foreign Armament Information. Human shadows behind the glass moved in waves across the semi-transparent surface.

With her hand on the knob of the door, she paused. Now was the moment of decision. Should she enter as Olga Diederich, the disgraced assassin, or as Adolph Leach, the interpreter? Well, she decided, I'll try first as Adolph, then, after I assess the situation, I can attempt to have them accept me as myself.

Resolutely turning the doorknob, Olga entered the anteroom just as a door to the left was closing. Opposite the closing door, a group of chairs were positioned against the wall. One stood empty; nervous-looking civil servant types occupied the other two. Looking straight ahead, Olga saw the counter where two stalwart ladies stood ready to question her about her business. The lighting overhead shined especially harsh at the counter and, as she approached, one of the stout ladies cocked her head in appraisal of Olga.

"I'm here on urgent and extremely sensitive business concerning 'stay-behind' army caches. Would you please direct me to the person who's in charge of such information?"

Both ladies raised their eyebrows at the young man's statement. Wasn't the last man—the one who had just left the waiting room and had entered the inner office—asking the same question? They seemed to be having a run on info about secret caches.

Intuitively sensing something wrong with the image of the young man standing before them—his face seemed too smooth, and the eyebrows were formed just so—one of the ladies said, "Would you remove your cap, young man, and take a seat over there. Someone will be with you shortly."

Disheartened, Olga turned and took the empty seat, still wearing the soggy cap. Feeling the gaze of the two ladies boring into her, she finally removed her cap, but left her hair in a straggly bun. She didn't look up at them, preferring to ignore the stir she must be causing.

At the counter, one of the ladies silently jabbed the other in the ribs. When her desk-mate turned to look at her, the other winked and nodded with an all-knowing smirk.

For Olga the warmth of the room and the sudden, forced inactivity made her acutely aware of how exhausted she felt. As the tension began to ebb out of her, her eyelids fluttered and grew heavy. Finally, after what seemed like half of an eternity, the door in front of her swung open, but no one came out. Instead, one of the stalwart ladies came from around the counter and motioned Olga to follow her inside the inner office. Then closing the door firmly, the lady turned abruptly and confronted the Stasi assassin.

"Would you like to amend your information, Fraulein? Adolph does not seem to fit your true identity now, does it? Unless, of course, your parents were devastated at not having you been born a baby boy. Or maybe, they were memorializing our deceased fuehrer. Which is it?"

"I'm in a race against time with my information, so the disguise was necessary."

"Well, it was a damn poor disguise. What male agent plucks his eyebrows?"

"It worked well enough for my purposes. In the gloom of

this weather, who can tell gender?"

"You must tell me your real name and anything else we need to identify you. Then you can take a seat and wait some more."

Back in the chair in the waiting room, Olga felt like she could weep. It was so darn frustrating. Then a question broke through her dark thoughts. Where had the person gone who had disappeared into the room as she was entering this office? Probably there was another exit. And, of course, there could be countless exits after the first one—exits ad infinitum until you found yourself out on the street or in a holding cell.

As Olga perched on the edge of the chair across from the large-headed man with wire-rimmed glasses sliding down his nose until they reached a bulbous impasse, she tried to calm her nerves. After all, she was finally in an office talking with an authority. Sliding to the back of the chair, she squared her shoulders and assumed a posture of confidence and repose. At the same time, the officer closed the file that had absorbed him and turned his gaze towards the assassin— ahem, failed assassin, he amended in his mind.

"You've had quite the busy time of it from Rome to Sardinia to Luxembourg, and finally here. I see that your specialty is assassinations. It says here you were successful in Rome in intercepting information which was about to be published in L'Osservatore Romano. That was the good news. The bad news was your capture by the CIA, along with the loss of one decoder, which allowed the CIA to insert its own mole in the system in order to thwart the assassination of Aldo Falucci. Did you learn anything from your stay in the prison at Capo Marrargui? Apparently, you did a fair job of breaking out of the prison, but you also left two of our agents behind. To be fair, they were not valuable agents—in fact rather dull—but they were nominally useful to us.

"Now I wonder what possessed you to flee to Luxembourg after breaking out of prison. One would think that you'd have stayed in Rome or come back to Berlin. At the very least, you could have contacted a Soviet agent in Rome so that we could have decided for you what your next operation would be." While saying this, the official reopened her file and scratched a few notes in the margins. At the end of writing each notation, the man made a question mark with a flourish that ended in a forcefully jabbed period. It was punctuation worthy of a high government functionary, thought Olga.

Slipping back towards the front of the chair, Olga leaned forward and looked at the man steadily. In a calm voice she began to set forth her argument.

"First of all, I failed in the assassination of Aldo Falucci because the CIA inserted a young nun in my place, who looked enough like me that people would have thought we were twins. She confused a lot of people. After I escaped from the prison, my first thought was to get rid of her so that my operating as an assassin could continue. I wanted nothing more than to serve my country and the Soviet Union.

"While in Rome, I learned my doppelganger might be Luxembourgish, so that's why I went there. Eventually, I found her." At this point, Olga paused in her narrative and considered that she didn't want to tell him yet how she had failed to kill her nemesis. Instead she moved on to the information she carried so religiously near her heart—the hidden armaments.

Now with more passion and excitement, she continued. "I came to your office because there's valuable information you should know about. It concerns hidden caches of armaments in Luxembourg City. No doubt, you've heard of the historic Casemates of that city which have earned it the title of 'Gibraltar of the North'. It truly is like Gibraltar. That is, it's a present day bastion. NATO has hidden an enormous amount of guns and ammunition in those caves. Why, the concept is brilliant, because not only are the caverns near an airport, but also near the most populated part of that little country. American and British troops could fly in and join the locally armed secret army in short order."

While Olga had been speaking faster and faster as she laid out her argument, the official proceeded to close his eyes, lean back and enlace his fingers across his substantial belly. Eventually, Olga realized her narrative was not getting the response she thought it would. Finally, running out of steam, she closed her mouth and waited.

Opening his eyes, the man said, "This is all old news to me. I know about those hidden armaments. You see, someone has beaten you to it." After a pause while he waited to see her reaction, he continued. "I believe you are familiar with Herr Oskar Feldmeier. He says that he had an intense encounter with you in Luxembourg—in fact in those very same caverns. After that encounter, he didn't know what had happened to you. But I knew you would turn up eventually. Anyone who had broken out of the Capo Marrargui prison and made her way back to Rome would not be put off by a small detail like an argument with another agent. You do have determination, I warrant."

Olga's gaze lost its intensity, and her shoulders slumped. She had lost the race; she was done. It seemed life had no meaning for her now, and it had all turned on a fenning. So much lost to her and so fast! Not even his notice of her determination could buoy her flagging spirits. She felt certain her future held some grueling discipline.

As the official rumbled on about her failings, depression and fatigue made her eyes sting and well up with tears. No, she thought, I will not show any weakness before this pompous ass. The memory came back to her clearly of how she felt when her Russian step-father had railed against her, and she would distract herself from shame by focusing on some object in the room.

Gazing over at the large desk before her, she concentrated on the shiny cylinder holding the official's collection of pens. One of them stood out as remarkable. It was an expensive Pelikan fountain pen with the Stasi emblem affixed to it. How proud he must be of it. Only a very well-esteemed Stasi member would have been given such a valuable gift.

After the official stopped his torrent of words, which included something about punishment and retraining, Olga rose from her chair. "Thank you for your time, sir. I don't believe I caught your name when I first came in."

The stout man looked annoyed at the coolness of this young woman before him. He harrumphed and finally stood up. Slightly tipped off–balance by his ample belly, he grabbed the edge of the desk for stability and attempted to stretch himself to his full height.

"My name is Herr Gherkinstein, Fraulein. But it should be of no concern to you!" Pressing a button on the intercom, he barked into it. "Frau Goetz, come and escort our visitor to the exit!"

Olga looked at him frostily, then reached into her backpack and extracted her hairbrush. Still focusing on his now frankly confused face, she undid her straggly bun and proceeded to brush her blonde hair into waves that flowed down her back.

When Frau Goetz entered the room and saw the scene, her mouth fell open as she tried to figure out just what was happening. As her gaze shifted from the young woman to her aging employer, she frowned in disapproval. Never in all of her years at headquarters had she seen anything like this! Most of the agents who were called into Herr Gherkinstein's office left it trembling and deflated—not making themselves more attractive.

Motioning for Olga to follow her, the stout matron opened the door to the other exit. With dignity, Olga followed as the matron led her down the long corridor to another elevator—a single elevator, which only went down.

Upon entering the elevator, Olga looked at the bank of buttons. It was strange. Not only did it only go down, but it had three minus numbers. Frau Goetz twisted her neck and looked up at the young agent. Slowly an evil smile spread across her face, but her eyes were as hard as granite. Abruptly, she turned back to the bank of buttons and punched minus three with relish.

Olga took a deep breath, looked steadily at the crack in the door where its two panels met in the middle and fingered the Stasi emblem on the Pelikan pen in her pocket. It was a souvenir worthy even of a failed assassin

.